THE COLLECTOR

GILLIAN ST. KEVERN

To Tui, the real life Cleo.

Seriously? I took you out five minutes ago.

Harbinger cast a bulging froglike eye over his register. He sat in a mahogany chair half again as tall as he was. A present from a grateful former client, as were the priceless mementoes dotted around the office. Once Harbinger had been butler to London's elite, dusting perhaps the same Chinese vase displayed on the mantel. Now he'd gone into business for himself, using his vast experience to match employers of pedigree with suitable servants. No judge presiding over a courthouse could give his sentence with more finality than Harbinger now. "As I thought, Mr Lawes. We have nothing suitable."

Gideon's palms were flat on his knees, braced for refusal. His nails dug into the fabric of his trousers. "I'm willing to try anything."

The words were a mistake. Harbinger stiffened, the already rigid muscles of his jaw shutting tight like a trap. "You appear to be under a misapprehension. The Harbinger agency prides itself on providing the most suitable of employees. You have an education, but that is all." He pushed Gideon's letters of reference back across the table. "You lack experience, breeding and the taste necessary to be a Harbinger's find."

Gideon's mouth was bitter. His ears rung as though boxed. "Taste?"

Harbinger sniffed, ringing the bell to signal his next visitor. "No servant worthy of the name would ever display desperation in public. Good day, Mr Lawes."

That was it then? Blaming the drowning man for not knowing how to swim? Gideon swallowed. Hysterical laughter was probably not on Harbinger's list of desirable qualities in an employee.

Harbinger had forgotten him already, bowing low as he greeted the newcomer. "Mr Westaway, this is a pleasant surprise."

The newcomer was a man of middle height, just pulling off his gloves. Despite the early hour, he wore an opera cape over his suit. "Pleasant is a matter of opinion, but surprise? This is my third visit this month."

It had been years since Gideon heard that light drawl, but it went under his skin like it was yesterday. Westaway. Naturally the man would show up just at the moment of Gideon's absolute disgrace. Well, he would not give him the pleasure of seeing him discomfited. He turned, his expression wooden.

Harbinger winced. "Burrowes did not give satisfaction? I have always considered him eminently suitable."

"I find no fault with his work." Westaway's strange amber eyes glanced over Gideon as he made room for him to pass. "My wardrobe has never been in better nick. No, it is as I told you last time. I need an unsuitable valet."

Westaway did not recognise him. Gideon walked out the door on legs that didn't seem to belong to him. His head spun. Was he so changed then? It had only been a couple of years since their matriculation.

A lot had happened in those years. Lawes breathed out. Just as well Westaway didn't know him. Their rivalry at Balliol consumed his undergraduate years. He'd only just beat Westaway to the first. Westaway seeing how far he'd fallen—intolerable! He must congratulate himself on his lucky escape.

A carriage rattled past, bulk passing only inches from him. Gideon jerked backwards. He caught his foot on a paving stone and looked around. He stood on a street corner. Good thing he'd paused. His present distracted mood was an accident waiting to happen.

It took Gideon a moment to recognise the street. Just how far had he walked? He smoothed his jacket down, feeling in his breast pocket. No references. He'd left them on Harbinger's desk.

Gideon's knees wobbled. He imagined Harbinger's sneer. "Recommend a man who cannot go five minutes without losing his references? You must see how impossible this is."

A hand closed on his shoulder.

Gideon jerked in surprise, spinning around. "I don't have any valuables, so it's no good—" His words died away. It was no street thug that accosted him.

Westaway watched him with the air of detachment that had so annoyed him in their undergraduate days. "Lost something, Lawes?" He held up a folded letter.

Gideon's cheeks burned. His references. "Thank you." He tucked the letter in his jacket pocket. Had Westaway seen them? "I didn't think you recognised me."

"I never forget people." Westaway pulled on his leather gloves. "Harbinger wouldn't approve of us throwing a reunion in his office. He's down on me enough as it is."

"Down on you?" Gideon's voice hitched. Westaway had money, connections, fame—an employer to boast of.

"I've rejected five suitable valets—or they've rejected me,

which comes to the same thing." Westaway shook out his opera cloak. "Harbinger can find a pair set of matched footmen at a day's notice. However, a man with full knowledge of the valet's art and a functioning imagination is beyond him. I've been told I must look elsewhere for my needs."

Harbinger had rejected Westaway too? What irony. Gideon pressed his lips together, striving for his old arrogance. "You won't find a suitable valet here." The note of scorn in his voice wasn't forced. Westaway's cloak had a furred collar and, even in the dim street, his buttons glittered like fool's gold. A visitor from the Arctic could not have looked any more out of place than he did.

"No," Westaway agreed. "Nor an unsuitable one." He hooked one gloved hand around Gideon's arm. "But I have found a companion for luncheon."

Gideon spluttered, partly from shock at Westaway's unbridled impudence, mostly from fear: he could not keep up his dignity much longer. "Luncheon?"

"I so hate dining alone," Westaway continued. "My treat."

"I'm a very busy man." Gideon tugged his arm away.

Westaway's grip remained inflexible. "There's a charming little bistro not two blocks from here. They do the most marvellous *coq au vin*. The chef assures me he only uses Burgundy wines in his cooking and the result backs him up. The most succulent chicken you've ever tasted, accompanied by hunks of salt pork, succulent mushrooms, all swimming in gravy."

"I—I already dined." A stale biscuit washed down with a cup of chicory was not dining, but it would have to do. Gideon's stomach gurgled.

Westaway cocked an eyebrow. "That didn't sound like indigestion. Come on. You got the first. Give me this." He tugged Gideon's arm.

He had no resistance left. Gideon let Westaway steer him across the street. Now that he'd won his point, he didn't chatter.

Thank God for minor mercies. The silence allowed Gideon the opportunity to collect his thoughts. A brief meal, perfunctory conversation satisfying the barest minimum of politeness, and he would be off. He hadn't tried all the banks yet. There must be one that needed a teller, or a clerk. Even a janitor.

The bistro was small and dim, far from the fashionable eatery Gideon had feared. He recognised no one.

The woman lounging against the counter brightened as they walked in. "Mr Westaway! Welcome. Is this a friend?"

"An old school fellow." Westaway let her take his cloak. "Happened on him by chance. The specialty of the house, and all the trimmings, Felicity. I want to make sure he doesn't get away."

She laughed, going to relay his order to the chef. Gideon, following Westaway to a table, thought it sounded too like the truth for his peace of mind. He caught the rich smells developing in the kitchen. How long had it been since he'd had anything resembling a full meal? He could not have walked out of the bistro, not if his dignity depended on it.

Westaway draped himself over the first chair and watched Gideon take his seat. "So, Lawes. What brought you to Harbingers?" His eyes raked over Gideon's suit. "Looking for a new valet?"

Noticing every worn patch and mended seam, just as Gideon had noticed Westaway's gaudiness. Gideon hunched in his seat. "The opposite. I let my man go. I'm economising." He never lied, but he could skirt around the truth.

"A sad day when you, the math genius, have to economise." Westaway tugged his gloves off, one finger at a time. "Didn't you land a cushy position for yourself at a bank? Barchester's. Junior partner." He brightened. "That was it, wasn't it?"

Westaway had remembered? Gideon clamped down on the strange fluttering in his chest. Westaway's memory had always been uncanny. This meant nothing. "Yes. That was it."

His tone must have given him away. Westaway looked up. "Past tense?"

Gideon nodded. He spoke fast, his voice clipped. Better do it now on his terms. "The bank failed. But not before I was dismissed."

Westaway sat up. "No one could think you had anything to do with that. You're the most honest chap I know—to your detriment."

Truer words. "I had something to do with it. Everything in fact. I noticed something wrong in—in rather a big way." He licked his lips. "Speculation by the other junior partner with the bank funds."

"Oh dear." Westaway's forehead creased. "And you told the senior partner?"

Gideon nodded. "It seemed the only right thing to do. He dismissed me. And it didn't seem like he was doing anything about it, so I told the chairman of the bank's board—"

"With the result that Barchester's is no more and your name is mud in London's banking circles."

Gideon winced. "I did what was right."

"You always were better at numbers than you were people. Banking in London is all about who you know, and Barchester Senior is a popular chap." Westaway's tone held no censure—and Gideon was listening for it.

"I couldn't have done anything else."

"No," Westaway agreed. "You're too honest for that. Although, that might be good."

"Good?" Gideon had always found Westaway unfathomable, but this was the limit.

"I speak entirely selfishly." His smile was mocking. Did he know what people said about him? "It just so happens that, besides an unsuitable valet, I'm in the market for a man of intelligence and scrupulous honesty. One who isn't afraid of ghosts."

2

G hosts? Gideon eyed Westaway. "If you're taking pity on me—"

Westaway held up a hand. "The favour would be conferred on me. But first, more important things." The woman returned bearing glasses and a bottle of wine, followed by the chef himself, carrying their meal. "Luncheon."

The *coq au vin* was everything Westaway promised and more. Gideon realised with horror it had been at least ten minutes without a word passing between them. Even hunger did not excuse such poor manners. He opened his mouth.

Westaway forestalled him. "A meal like this requires one's complete attention. We'll talk afterwards."

Gideon complied without protest. Stomach full, he leaned back in his chair, content stealing over him. Westaway had laid his trap well. He was comfortable, too comfortable to want to stir.

Westaway watched him. The muted interior took the edge off his eyes, turning them an ordinary brown rather than their usual off-putting shade. His gaze made Gideon self-conscious. That was the devil of Westaway. Even the most casual of glances had intent behind it. The man was so cursed hard to decipher.

Gideon disliked puzzles. "You said you needed an honest man?"

Westaway inclined his head. "You've not met my father, have you?"

"I have not had that pleasure."

Westaway snorted. "He is a man of peculiar—one might say eccentric—interests. I curb his excesses where I can."

Gideon made a polite noise and kept his expression blank. Westaway curbing anyone's impulses was pure nonsense. Just look at that cloak!

"His current mania is haunted houses," Westaway continued. "He's found one with a marked reputation for noises and accidents and is eager to make an offer. I've persuaded him to investigate first. I've rented the place for a quarter. The problem is investigating it. Father's health isn't the best, and while fond of him, I draw the line at moving into squalid, rat-infested apartments to indulge his curiosity."

"But you would have me live there." Did he grasp the situation aright?

Westaway's smile was ironic. "I would compensate you for the inconvenience. While my tenant, I will supply you with all you need in terms of furnishings and equipment, in addition to your salary."

Gideon leaned in. "You'd pay me to live in this house?"

"I need you to record anything unusual that happens in the house," Westaway said. "Footsteps, strange creaks, everything. I am relying on your scrupulous honesty and note-taking ability. That hasn't changed since our Balliol days, has it?"

"No. It has not." Westaway couldn't be serious. "I don't believe in ghosts."

"That may be an advantage." Westaway picked a thread

off his sleeve. "You wouldn't feel strange in a haunted house?"

Gideon shook his head. "All old houses have noises." The boarding house he lodged in creaked in the slightest breeze, but he'd not once imagined ghosts. "Logic can account for any other phenomena. Plumbing, or those rats you mentioned."

"The rats are of more practical concern. Come along and see the place," Westaway suggested. "It's walking distance. Unless you've got somewhere you need to be?"

The thought of walking to yet another bank to endure yet another dismissal was too much. Westaway was not sympathetic, but he wasn't pitying either. Gideon's other acquaintances either cut him once the news of Barchester's collapse broke, or greeted him with a too-hearty manner, as if to assure him they did not view him differently. Westaway's manner was actually unchanged. They might be sharing a table in the college dining hall. He craved not Westaway's company but his normalcy. "No harm in looking at the place."

Westaway's face gave no sign of pleasure. "I'll settle our bill and then we'll be on our way."

As the woman brought Westaway his cloak, she held up a thin black band. "This fell when you removed your cloak. Can I just say how sorry we are?"

Westaway's mouth twisted. "We all are." He walked out of the restaurant before anyone could say another word.

Gideon followed. Westaway set a fast pace. He jogged after him at a pace their lunch made difficult. "Thought the better of your offer, Westaway? You need not flee from me if so."

Westaway stopped still. "I beg your pardon." Once Gideon caught up, he continued at a more moderate pace. "I wasn't thinking of it at all and the reminder stung."

Gideon wasn't expecting explanation—especially one so honest. It didn't seem decent. "Understandable."

Westaway stared straight ahead. "Your company took me back to old times. It was six months ago now."

The same time as Barchester's collapse. Westaway hadn't known then? Gideon hesitated. Could he ask…

"Lord Cross."

Gideon frowned. "Your sponsor?"

"More, much more, than that. He was a dear friend of my father's and a second father to me." Westaway's frown deepened. "It seems wrong there isn't a better word for what he was to us, but human language is so lacking." Gideon's expression must have shown his discomfit. Westaway grimaced. "I'm being too personal, aren't I?"

"Not at all." Cross had visited his charge a few times at Oxford. The college welcomed him with all the pomp and ceremony due to an old boy of his rank. Gideon had sneered at this further evidence of Westaway's affectations, but found the tall, sharp eyed man an intimidating prospect. Westaway's ability to maintain breezy good humour in the face of Cross's marked ill-temper was impressive. Had he genuinely been fond of such a waspish man? "Was it sudden?"

"Very. An accident, and if you don't mind, we'll leave it at that." Westaway motioned to the street sign ahead of them. "Belcairn Road. This is it, my lad."

Did Westaway know his casual 'my lads' grated, or was that coincidence? Bristling, Gideon looked down a row of Tudor townhouses. These were not the decrepit wrecks of Wych Street. Pains were taken to plaster over cracks and replace beams, sweep front steps and plant flowers in window boxes.

"Not the most fashionable of neighbourhoods." Westaway strolled down the ample footpath. "Your neighbours are in trade, a quiet, industrious bunch according to the agent. Here we are. The black sheep of the street."

32 Belcairn Road was dingier than its neighbours. The windows were dim with dust. In place of a doormat, the front step had a thick collection of coal dust.

Westaway pulled a large brass key from his pocket and twisted it in the doorknob. "I won't tell you anything of the place. Don't want to give you any false impressions, you know. Just see if you think you can stick it."

Gideon nodded and pushed the door open.

It took a few moments for his eyes to adjust to the dim interior. Dark wood panels lined the walls. The air was stale, and there was a faint odour of animal, but he could not smell any damp.

Westaway struck a match, using it to light one of two candle holders set on a low chest by the entrance. He held one out to Gideon.

Gideon took the candle holder and tried the first door. It opened with a slight creak into a sitting room containing a sizeable fireplace, two empty bookcases, a row of glass bottles, some moth-eaten chairs and a sofa. The curtains hung in tatters, but despite the obvious neglect, Gideon liked the room at once. "This would make a capital study." He ran a hand over the back of the sofa. How long had it been since he'd had a study of his own?

Westaway glanced at him. "I believe it was, once. The house was a bachelor establishment—there I go, doing what I shouldn't."

They explored the other rooms on the first floor: a dining room with the great table still there (as Westaway pointed out, impossible to get it through the doors), a second sitting room, the kitchen, cellar, and servant's room, all filled with an astonishing amount of detritus. On the second floor, there were three bedrooms, another room for a servant, and a ladder to the attic. The smell of rats was strongest there.

"Well, Lawes." They stood in the master bedroom. Westaway prodded the bed and watched the dust rise. "This is a lot to inflict on a chap. What do you think?"

It would not do to seem eager. Gideon tugged his collar. "Getting this place habitable will take a lot of work."

"I'll manage that. The agent has a woman come in every week to give the place a quick going over, keep it from getting run down. She's willing to be your daily."

Gideon swallowed bile. There it was. "I—"

"I'll engage her on your behalf. Since this is my undertaking, only fair I foot the bill." Westaway pulled the curtains aside and, after a moment's struggle, heaved the window up. "Will you need a man, do you think?"

"I don't think so. My needs are modest."

"I was thinking of company. You'll find the house lonely."

It could not be lonelier that his room in the boarding house, where no one gave each other a 'good morning.' Honest silence would be a relief. "You've forgotten my solitary habits."

"If you're sure." Westaway turned aside from the window. "The neighbours seem decent folk. They'd give you a hand should you need it."

"And all you'd have me do is record my impressions of the place?"

Westaway nodded. "You sound like you're considering it."

Gideon inclined his head. "I think it a foolish commission and don't see the point… But I am at a loose end and need something to occupy myself with. You mentioned a salary?"

Westaway named his sum.

Gideon clutched the bedpost. "That is generous." There was a catch here.

"Most people require an inducement to stay in a haunted house." Westaway shoved the window down again. "I've got an appointment with my tailor. Think of the matter tonight and write me tomorrow with your answer."

"I know my mind."

"I would prefer you take time to consider it," Westaway said. "There's no rush. I have the house for a quarter."

Strange that of the two of them, it was self-indulgent, fickle Westaway who urged waiting. Following Westaway down the stairs, Gideon frowned. How well did he know him? How much of Westaway's manner was poise, and what real—

He stumbled forward, catching the bannister just in time to avoid a collision.

Westaway spun around, placing a hand on Gideon's arm. "All right?"

Gideon looked behind him. The corridor stood empty. He sucked in a sharp breath. "No harm done."

"The stairs are narrow. I must see if we can't have a light here—it's dim." Westaway continued down the stairs.

After a moment, Gideon followed. His heart beat a fast but steady alarm in his chest. The dim light didn't cause him to miss the step. He'd felt a quick sharp shove, right in the middle of his back. Someone had pushed him.

3

The two lightermen who shared the room next to Gideon's elected that night for a drawn-out quarrel, making sleep impossible. His breakfast of tepid under-brewed tea and congealing kippers decided him. Odd incident on the stairs aside, he would accept Westaway's ridiculous offer.

He wrote to Westaway's address and delivered the letter himself. The footman mistook Gideon for a messenger and tipped him. Insulting, but it was a cup of hot coffee and a muffin fresh out of the oven. Was his luck changing?

A week later, he was once again in the downstairs study of 32 Belcairn Road. This time, a fire crackled in the grate. Gideon watched it from one of Westaway's armchairs. He'd sent around some furniture from his own townhouse. He'd also supplied reading matter, filled the coal cellar, stocked the larder, had all the rooms scrubbed from top to bottom, the windows cleaned, the curtains replaced, and fresh mattresses and linen placed in two of the bedrooms.

This Gideon had protested. "What good is a second bedroom to me? I told you, I have no man."

"You may wish to entertain a guest," Westaway said. "If so, you'll need somewhere to sleep them."

As Westaway had also provided a few bottles of rather fine madeira from his cellar, Gideon let that pass without further comment.

The last of Westaway's excesses was curled up before the crackling fire. The terrier basked, eyes closed, belly exposed to the warmth. She was short of hair, with an intelligent face and alert brown eyes. The man who'd delivered her assured Gideon that she was a champion rat hunter. He had yet to see anything of the hunter's disposition. So far the dog seemed inclined to either indolence or affection.

As if feeling his eyes upon her, the dog turned her head, resting melting brown eyes upon him. Her tail beat the floor.

"All right." Gideon snapped his fingers.

The dog leaped to her feet, padding over to stand beneath his hand. He gave her a scratch beneath her chin. "Champion rat hunter, my foot. You're spoilt rotten, that's what you are." The dog closed her eyes, her tail a steady blur. "Then again, I'm spoilt too. All this to watch a house."

Westaway's proposal made no more sense now, but having partaken of his hospitality, Gideon knew his duty. He gave the dog a final scratch and seated himself at the writing desk.

Well, Westaway,

If this is how you treat all your tenants, you are the most generous landlord in existence. So far, your preparations are for nothing. I write to tell you I am comfortably settled and that my first evening in 32 Belcairn Road has passed without incident.

·   ·   ·

Gideon paused. Was it without incident?

One of your hired men might have met with serious accident had it not been for the quick reflexes of his fellows. He caught his foot coming down the stairs and fell. If his friend had not forestalled him, he might have done himself a serious injury. As it was, he sprained his ankle. I gave him a guinea from the money you left for house repairs as he won't be able to work until his ankle heals.

Gideon stared at the paper. It wasn't his use of Westaway's funds that worried him. He shied away from putting the thought into words. He didn't want Westaway to think he was making assumptions…

Something wet pressed against his hand.

Gideon jerked upright, pen stabbing into the paper.

The dog looked at him, her eyes affronted. As Gideon stared down at her, she nosed his hand again. Wanting to be petted.

Gideon shut his eyes, breathing out. "Of all the fool things…" Not even one night in the house and he was as nervy as if he believed in spirits. He turned back to the paper.

Matter of fact, it was the same step that I stumbled on last week. Clearly something wrong with the stairs. I shall have a carpenter in to look at it and in the meantime make it a rule to never go downstairs without a firm hand on the bannister. Of sinister noises, doors opening of their own accord and phantom echoes, I can make no report.

I will write again in the morning, but for now, I shall bid you good night.

. . .

He rose, tucking the paper into his pocket. He stroked the terrier's ears and then snapped his fingers. "Come on." The kitchen door opened on a dank yard. Grimy weeds sprouted in the cracks between mottled paving stones. He could not imagine a more cheerless yard, yet the terrier gave it full consideration, sniffing every stone twice before fixing on a spot for her deposits.

Gideon averted his eyes. His thoughts reverted to the absurdity of the situation. He—Gideon Lawes, who had beaten Westaway to the first—keeping house for him! Was Westaway smirking over a glass of champagne somewhere, picturing this very scene?

The dog scratched at the door, ready to retire.

Gideon opened the door. "Here, girl." He would have to think of a name for her. It was about the only thing Westaway hadn't provided. His foresight had extended as far as the rough blanket folded in a corner of the study to be the terrier's bed.

Gideon pointed at the blanket. "Bed."

The dog looked at the blanket and her tail drooped. She turned her head back to Gideon. She wagged her tail.

"No," Gideon said. "You sleep here." He shut the study door and climbed up the stairs.

Halfway up the stairs, he heard a whine. A pitiful scratch at the door followed.

Gideon raised his voice. "Go to bed."

He climbed the rest of the stairs. He'd never had a dog before. Perhaps he should have asked the man who brought her how old she was? If she was a puppy and this her first house…

No, even a puppy must learn to sleep alone. Taking a firm hand was the key. Gideon did not intend to waste his time in

Belcairn Road. He had letters of enquiry to frame, and a treatise on mathematics to pen. Spending time with Westaway had brought back college associations, and with them a new avenue of hope. No bank would employ him, but perhaps a school, as a teacher of mathematics?

If he wanted to teach, he'd need to contribute an article to some journal of scholarly standing to take the taint of commercialism from his name. Westaway had won the essay prize, but Gideon had made him work hard for it. He could pen something worth printing. The only question was what?

Belatedly, with the covers pulled up to his chin, he realised he'd extinguished his candle before he'd made a thorough search of the room. A precaution, in case the ghost had an all too physical form.

The bed was comfortable—too comfortable for Gideon to want to quit it. Snug within his many blankets, Gideon snorted. How anyone could imagine a bedroom this comfortable haunted was beyond him! Westaway had the right idea. All the place needed was proper furnishing. Gideon wouldn't mind living there permanently…

He was just on the edge of sleep when a door opened downstairs.

Gideon lay still.

The room was quiet. He stilled his breathing, ears straining.

Had he really heard a door? Gideon rehearsed his steps that evening. After dinner, he'd made a tour of the house, securing every window and closing every door. He'd even checked every cupboard. No, imagination—

The stair creaked.

Gideon swallowed.

Another creak. Another. Whatever made the sounds was drawing closer.

Shuffling sounds in the corridor. It knew the way to his

room, not even hesitating. In a moment—yes, there it was, the dread sound of the door swinging open.

"What do you mean by this intrusion?" Gideon grappled for the candle. He struck the match, and by its glare saw the doorway was empty.

Gideon stared at the door across the hall. He remembered the match just in time to avoid scorching his fingertips. He lit the candle and raised the candle holder.

No one in the doorway. No one in the hall either. Gideon stood in the doorway, listened.

The house creaked, the pressure of the night breezes outside. Nothing more than that. Gideon pulled the door closed.

He stood in the centre of his room. He had not imagined the door opening. Nor had he felt a draught of any kind in the hall, and he'd heard the wind only after the door had swung open. How to explain this?

He heard the creak, noticed the presence beside him too late to escape it.

A warm head pressed against his leg. Gideon looked down into the hopeful eyes of the terrier. She wagged her tail.

4

―――――――――

For a man spending the night in a haunted house, Gideon slept well. He woke once or twice for no apparent reason, a fact he put down to nerves. "The power of suggestion," he told the dog. "I hand it to Westaway. He knew what he was about, not giving me the story of the place. Had he told me, the noises last night would have matched to perfection the scrape of a wooden leg down the corridor or the moans of an abandoned widow—whatever the ghost is."

The dog nestled further into the blankets Gideon had occupied.

"Shameless." Gideon tugged his tie straight and pulled his jacket sleeves down. "Don't even have the grace to be embarrassed of the way you acted last night. Creeping in uninvited." He'd reasoned leaving the dog downstairs would be more trouble than leaving her on the bed, a decision the events of the night had borne out. The dog was satisfied to sleep at the foot of the bed. How she'd migrated to be curled next to him when he woke was a mystery, but one Gideon was content to leave unsolved for now.

He glanced once at himself in the mirror of the open wardrobe. His meagre belongings looked inadequate within the cavernous wardrobe. A reminder that his presence wasn't permanent. Better get started on that essay. He snapped his fingers. "Come on, girl."

The terrier stretched and dropped onto the floor with all the lightness of a cat. She padded down the hallway and stairs, tail held high, coming to a pause beside the kitchen door.

Gideon smiled as he followed. Did she consider him her master or her door opener?

The harsh sound of a brush on stone indicated that Mrs Lightfoot was within. Gideon steeled himself, summoning what he hoped was a winning smile. "Ah, Mrs Lightfoot. Good morning."

She sniffed, the sound rattling deep within her sinuses. "Good morning, you say! Plain to see you haven't been up half the night with a cough."

Gideon winced. "You're not too unwell, I trust?"

"No worse than usual." She heaved herself upright, ending somewhere around Gideon's elbow. She was a slight woman. Even her skirts lacked volume, clinging to her thin form like leaves on a wilted plant. She spoke in a harsh whisper, with a cough rattling the back of her throat or the suggestion of something moist and unpleasant brewing. She was less a charwoman, more a collection of ailments. That said, she did for Gideon with surprising energy. "My back's acting up again. Didn't I tell you it would? Those damp cellar stones always put my back out."

"You mentioned your back." And her gammy knee, bad eye and the twinge in her stomach. "Perhaps we can leave the cellar. I'm not likely to use it much."

"No," Mrs Lightfoot agreed. "Not much for the cellar is the ghost."

Gideon changed the subject. Better to keep a blank slate. "Is that herring for me?"

She nodded. "Lovely bit of fish, that is. Fried and with a

nice cup of tea, that will do you for breakfast—tuppence fresh."

A reminder he had not paid her housekeeping? "Capital. I shall get out of your way." Gideon made his escape before she could start on her bad joints.

He left the dog nosing around the corners of the kitchen and retreated to the study. He took out the pouch Westaway had left for expenses. As he counted out the coins for Mrs Lightfoot, one slipped to the floor. Gideon set the stack of coins on his desk and went after the errant coin. It had rolled all the way across the floor. As Gideon knelt to pick it up, he noticed scratches in the door.

"That nuisance dog!" Not one night in Westaway's house and she had damaged it. Gideon ran a hand over the marks. Not too deep. That was something, at least. He could sand it down and find some stain, make it good as new. He would have to tell Westaway of the matter. He stood. That settled it. He would not leave the dog alone in a room by herself—

Turning back to his desk, Gideon got a second shock. His neat stack of coins was gone.

"They were just here." He lifted aside the books on the table, but the coins were nowhere in sight. He placed the coin he'd just picked up on the table and scanned the room. Had he dropped them into his pocket? He patted his trousers and his jacket without success.

Maybe he'd only thought he'd put the coins down on the table? Gideon opened the pouch, totalling up the coins contained within. No—he'd taken out Mrs Lightfoot's wages and the amount due for expenses. He counted out the amount a second time, turning to collect the errant penny.

Nothing there.

Gideon stared at the desk. Once was strange enough, but this… This was downright peculiar. "There must be a logical explanation." There had not been time for anyone to sneak into the room and take the coins. They must be there.

A brief search revealed that they weren't.

Mrs Lightfoot entered the room while Gideon was still on his hands and knees beneath the desk. "Lost something, Mr Lawes?"

Gideon sat back on his heels. "Matter of fact, yes."

Mrs Lightfoot held a teapot on a tray. "Money, was it?"

Gideon stood. "Why yes, but how you knew that—"

"You won't be seeing that again." She snuffled. "Ghost has an easy hand where money's concerned."

Gideon peered at her. "First I've ever heard of a light-fingered ghost."

"You put that in your report to Mr Westaway. Tell him your money's gone—and you can give me my wages in the kitchen." A hacking cough shook her entire frame. "Begging your pardon for speaking so plain."

"The ghost doesn't have much to do with the kitchen?" Gideon held up his hand. "No, don't tell me. Let's go to the kitchen."

In the kitchen, he counted out the coins in the pouch for the third time, handing Mrs Lightfoot her due. "I'm sure there's some other explanation. Animal, perhaps. Magpies steal shiny objects."

Mrs Lightfoot set the tray of tea things down on the kitchen table with a rattling cough. "Did you see a magpie in the study? Because I didn't. Nor an open window. And I always notice open windows on account of my bad chest."

Was there a part of her that wasn't bad? "A rat then."

"I'd like to see that rat that could sneak a pile of coins from under your nose." Mrs Lightfoot wasted no time wrapping her salary in a handkerchief and depositing it in the depths of her apron pocket.

She had an excellent point. He hadn't been on his hands and knees that long…

A loud crash made Gideon jump. "What was that?"

Another crash followed. "Good heavens—it sounds like the study!"

"You've set him off," Mrs Lightfoot observed. "Not much to do now but wait till he's done." She pulled out a chair from the kitchen table and removed a pipe from her pocket. "Got any tobacco?"

Gideon strode to the door and pulled it open. Another smaller crash—the sound of toppling furniture. The noises came from the vacated study. Gideon seized the door handle.

"It's locked!"

"There's no getting in," Mrs Lightfoot droned from the doorway. "Not till he's finished, leastways."

Gideon rattled the handle and pounded on the door. "You in there, open this door!"

"Wasting your breath," Mrs Lightfoot said. "I'll give you your breakfast in the kitchen."

"I demand you open this door!" No answer was forthcoming. Gideon rammed the door with his shoulder. Hissing, he repeated the attempt.

The door clicked open. He staggered into the room. All about him, chairs and side tables were upended, the paper on his desk scattered across the room. "How dare you intru—" The words died on his lips. The room was empty of any person save himself.

5

After pocketing the coins, the 'ghost' rifled through my papers and turned the study furniture upside down, tossing cushions aside and knocking over chairs. No animal did this. No, I suspect a common thief who has found the supernatural a convenient guise to mask his activities. How he manages his entrance and exit is so far a mystery. The only way out of the room are the door which I was at, the windows which were closed from the inside, and the chimney which shows no sign of being disturbed.

Gideon weighed the words he'd just written. He imagined Westaway smirking over his confusion. Intolerable.

The ghost has a taste for the finer things in life. A few hours after the disturbance, Mrs Lightfoot realised that she'd missed an opportunity for histrionics. She 'came down all of a quiver' and demanded 'a stiffener.' Since the cellar would wreak havoc on her joints, I went to retrieve a glass of your very excellent madeira. The bottle that had been half full the night before was drained and a second opened. Should I suspect the 'ghost' or the charwoman? For all her ailments, she moves fast when the dog tries to gain entrance to the pantry.

Gideon tapped the nib of his pen on the blotting paper. Were the 'ghost' and Mrs Lightfoot in league? The charwoman spreading word about the ghost to give him cover for his activities, perhaps? No—there was nothing to attract a thief in this empty house. The few coins stolen by the ghost were not equal recompense for the effort the man took to steal them. What then was his motive?

Gideon strode over to the window. Even at this late hour of the day, the street was in shadow, the overhanging eaves of the houses opposite preventing the sun from lightening the gloom. The surrounding houses shared the same air of depression. The ghost was not interested in real estate, and if he were, why choose an empty house for his activities? By Westaway's accounts, the landlord was keen to sell.

Was the house's desertion the appeal? A den for thieves... Gideon shook his head, turning away from the window. The house had shown no prior signs of occupation...

The terrier snuffled in a corner.

"What have you found, girl?" Gideon squatted beside her, peering beneath an antique press too heavy to remove. A scrap of paper lay beneath.

Dropped by the thief? Gideon lay flat on the floor, stretching his arm out. It took some undignified wriggling, but at last his fingers closed on the crinkled edges of the scrap. He drew his prize into the light.

His heart sank. Faded ink adorned yellowed paper. His thief hadn't dropped that. The paper had been under the press for years.

The dog barked. She stood by the door. As Gideon looked up, her tail wagged.

"You want to go out?" Gideon dropped the paper into his

pocket and opened the door. Instead of going to the kitchen which led to the yard, the terrier trotted over to the front door. "A walk? Not a bad idea." Gideon scratched her ears. "I'll finish that letter to Westaway, and we can post it on the way."

Listen to him, talking to a dog as if she understood! Gideon grimaced as he sat down at the writing desk. Maybe Westaway was right, and he needed company... He dashed off a few concluding sentences and folded, addressed and stamped the letter. The dog danced around him as he pulled on his coat and hat.

"Anyone would think you hadn't been out of the house in weeks." Gideon opened the door, and she shot outside. A cat? No—she made for the lamppost, a favourite with the neighbourhood dogs. Gideon strolled down the street, raising his hat to a passing housewife. The terrier would follow.

She did. They enjoyed a brisk circuit of the neighbouring park, posting Westaway's letter on the way. Gideon unlocked the door of the house a happier man. "We must do this more often," he told the terrier. "The break is pleasant."

She, ever optimistic, darted into the kitchen to see if there were any scraps left in her plate. Gideon divested himself of coat and hat and opened the study door.

Someone had ransacked the room, opening the drawers of his desk and spilling its contents across the floor.

For a moment, Gideon stared at the mess. Windows shut, chimney undisturbed, front door locked... He walked into the kitchen to test the back door, already knowing what he would find. He'd locked it behind Mrs Lightfoot when she left.

She had a key. She could have returned after he'd left or lent her key to someone else. Could there be a third key in someone else's possession? "I must ask the rental agency."

For now, however, Gideon rolled up his sleeves. For the second time that day, he put the room to rights.

He'd just about finished when the terrier barked. Gideon looked out of the study door to see her standing by the front door, quivering with fury. She snarled, planted in front of the door, like a tiny sentinel sounding the alarm.

"What is it girl?" An envelope was pressed through the mail slot and a crisp knock followed. "The mailman?" He picked up the envelope. A reply from Westaway already?

My dear Lawes,

I should get that carpenter in sooner rather than later and be very careful on those stairs. You did the right thing compensating the workman. Let me know if you run low on money for expenses—and on the subject of money, it might be wise to keep yours in your bedroom.

Gideon raised an eyebrow. Had Westaway known of the ghost's apparent predilection?

Should you desire some company, my club is at your disposal. I've included my card. The beef stew is above average.

Julian Westaway.

Gideon tapped the card. He did not want to be any further in Westaway's debt, but a beef stew sounded much more tempting than the sausages Mrs Lightfoot had left for his dinner.

His stomach growled. "Fine, Westaway. You win—again. But I will have the last laugh."

The terrier protested being left behind, doing her best to dart out the door with him. Gideon resorted to the undignified stratagem of feigning indifference and then sneaking out the back door. As he locked the kitchen door behind him, a chill penetrated the scarf looped around his coat neck. He caught the brisk scent of strong tobacco. He looked up, but he was alone in the stone-paved yard.

"Hello?" Gideon rattled the door of the little shed—not opened in years, the key lost and no one caring enough to remove the bolt and padlock from its front—but did not get a response. There was nowhere else in the bare yard for anyone to conceal themselves. The smoker must have just left by the gate.

Gideon seized the gate, expecting to throw it open. Instead, he collided with thick wooden planks. "Oof!" He stumbled back, rubbing his shoulder. Locked. And stubbornly locked, too. He fought to get the key to turn in the disused lock. When he heaved the gate open, it disclosed years of grime beneath.

Gideon shouldered the gate back into place. The smoke must have travelled on the breeze. He looked up, but the windows of the neighbouring houses were shut. He didn't remember hearing a closing window... "Get a hold of yourself." Gideon pulled his coat tighter around himself. "It's the only explanation."

6

G ideon had passed the brick entranceway and black painted door at number fourteen Wilding Street many times without giving it a second thought. He knocked, conscious of the tightness in his chest. What would be on the other side?

This was Westaway's club. He must share it with friends —friends who might remember Gideon from their school days. His heart sank. Perhaps he'd be better off cooking sausages with the ghost?

"It's not a ghost—oh, I beg your pardon."

The door swung open. An impeccably attired doorman with an expectant manner stood within. "Yes?"

Gideon held out Westaway's card.

"Mr Lawes. We've been expecting you." The superior personage returned the card to Gideon and motioned him inside. "Mr Westaway dines upstairs in the private restaurant."

Private sounded promising. Less chance of seeing anyone he knew. "That suits me."

"Follow me." The doorman strode down the hallway.

Gideon followed him down a dim hallway, breathing in

sandalwood and beeswax. Number fourteen had not made the shift to gas lighting, the corridor lit by wax candles at regular intervals.

The closed doors had brass plates reserving them for various groups. The Society of Midnight Masons. The Lepidopterist Collective. The Daylight Club. The Phasmatological Society. An open door on his right revealed a comfortable lounge well provided with fireplaces and armchairs. Gideon saw himself occupying one of those later. For now, he climbed the stairs after the doorman.

The hallmark of the dining room seemed to be 'discretion.' Tables stood at generous intervals and diners spoke in murmurs. The footman led Gideon to a table marked 'reserved.' A table in the private dining room was not enough, no—Westaway must have a private table. "Are you expecting Westaway to dine tonight?"

"I believe Mr Westaway is in the country." The footman removed the card, but not before Gideon had seen the text: *For use by members of the Phasmatological Society and their guests.* "We do things differently here, Mr Lawes. There is no menu, but our cook can produce most anything that is requested."

Anything? What, was he expecting Westaway to be a member of a normal club? "I've been recommended to try your beef stew."

"Very good, sir." The doorman bowed.

Gideon tugged at his collar. "What is the Phasmatological—"

The footman had already departed.

Gideon straightened the cutlery on the table and looked out the window. He had a bird's-eye view of the street, but the angle of the window masked him from the view of pedestrians. In the street below, a woman straightened her hat in the club's curtained windows then, after a quick glance to determine she was alone, adjusted her bodice.

Gideon looked away, his cheeks flaming. He cast around for something to distract him. He pulled the receipt he'd picked up beneath the press and out of his pocket. Rubbish, no doubt. He smoothed it out.

It was not, as he'd first thought, a receipt. Rather, someone appeared to be working out a budget. The amount at the top was their income, followed by a series of deductions and an ever decreasing total…

Gideon winced as he looked to the bottom of the paper. He and the owner of the paper were in similar financial straits. He'd worked out his own budget following the same method, starting with his rent—that must be it there, the biggest expense—followed by food, the recurring charge there…

Gideon frowned. The owner of the paper had done a poor job of his sums. He'd made a serious error in his first subtraction—and that was far from the only mistake. Gideon felt in his jacket for a pencil. Nothing—he'd left it on his desk.

"Excuse me." A man stood at Gideon's elbow. His black hair was sleek and moulded to his skull. His aftershave wafted towards Gideon in a wave. "Are you aware that this is a private table?"

"Yes, thank you," Gideon said. "I am."

His brown eyes flashed. "A private table reserved for a select group of people." His eyes dropped to Gideon's suit.

Gideon tugged at his collar. "I gathered."

The man stared at him. "A select group you're not a part of."

Gideon's skin tingled as if struck. He discovered his throat too tight to speak. He held out Westaway's card.

The man glanced at it. His elegant sneer vanished, and he clutched the table as if he needed the support. "You're not— Westaway couldn't prefer your company."

Gideon retrieved the card from trembling fingers. "I

wouldn't pretend to know anything about Westaway's preferences, but I am expecting to dine alone."

The man folded into the chair opposite. "You're not friends? No—of course not." The shock was fading, his eyes losing their glassiness. He tugged at one end of a scanty handlebar moustache, attempting his former superior manner. "Are you one of his father's curiosities?"

Gideon's forehead throbbed. "I know Westaway from our Oxford days."

The other man's brow narrowed. "I suppose one can't choose one's schoolfellows, but even so… What are you doing here?"

Would it be too much to hope that if he answered the man's questions, he would go? "I was hoping to dine, but if you must know, I'm investigating a house at Westaway's request."

"Investigating a house." The man pursed his lips, sharp eyes again flicking over Gideon. "His latest intrigue is serious then?"

Gideon blinked. "I beg your pardon?"

"If he's going to the effort of housing his paramour, then it's not an ordinary dalliance." The man smiled at Gideon's expression. "I know all about Westaway's little intrigues, believe me."

He reminded Gideon of a cat waiting for the least expected moment to break out its claws. "I assure you, you are mistaken."

"No need to be coy." The man leaned in, his voice smooth as whiskey. "Let's just say that I am…intimately familiar with Westaway's habits."

He seemed to expect a reaction. "How jolly for you."

The man stared back at him, a puzzled expression in his eyes. "Are you—"

A throat cleared. A white-haired man in faded tweeds looked down at the dark-haired man, his expression stern. "I believe this table is for society members and their guests only."

The dark-haired man scowled. "Rupert Pettifog. Remember me." He stomped off, only just avoiding colliding with a waiter.

Gideon swallowed. He was not looking forward to justifying his presence at the table a second time. "I beg your pardon. I—"

"Mr Lawes?" the white-haired man said. "Do you mind if I join you?" He spoke with a curious accent, an Irish lilt to his words, but his vowels were nasal. A colonial?

"Please." Gideon motioned to the vacated chair.

He sat, unwinding his scarf and revealing a dog collar beneath. "Please forgive the intrusion. You seemed in need of rescuing."

"Thank you," Gideon said and meant it. "I've got no idea why Mr Pettifog took such umbrage at my presence."

"Don't you?" The man's eyes were a muted green. Like Pettifog's they roamed over Gideon, but he didn't feel judged. "But then, it has been some time since you last saw Julian." He smiled at Gideon's expression. "I know all about your task, Mr Lawes. In fact, if you hadn't volunteered, I should have been the next recruit. I'm Julian's godfather, you see."

"Godfather?" What on earth was Westaway doing with something so mundane as a godfather?

"I can't blame your surprise," the white-haired man continued. "I have so little influence over Julian one would assume he had no godfather at all. But for all his faults, he is a charming companion and a loyal son."

This was just as awkward as Pettifog's bewildering conversation. "Then you know about the house?"

"I know about the house." The man paused.

A waiter set two steaming bowls of stew in front of them. "Beef stew, Father O'Connor."

"This will do nicely, Granger." O'Connor smiled at the

waiter. He waited until he was across the room before resuming the conversation. "The house is the reason I'm here tonight. I hoped I might catch you. I'm curious how it's going."

Gideon gave a shaky laugh. "I can't say it's not been interesting."

The priest made an excellent listener. Gideon felt better after unburdening himself, and the warm stew completed the cure. As he laid down his fork, he felt ashamed at his lack of endurance. "Time for me to return. Thank you for your company, Father O'Connor. I enjoyed our conversation."

"You're returning then?" O'Connor stroked his chin.

"Where else would I go?"

O'Connor's brow furrowed. "There are always other options. In fact, there is a spare bed in my hotel room."

"That's very kind of you father, but Westaway is expecting me to do a job, and I will do the job."

"He would understand if you wished to stay elsewhere. The circumstances of having an intruder not once, but twice..."

Gideon shook his head. "A man is only as good as his word. I've never lied, not once. If I say I'll do a thing, I'll do it."

O'Connor frowned. "I see I cannot dissuade you. However, would you object to a houseguest?"

"You?"

"I have some experience in these matters, and I'll admit, some curiosity."

"Then you're welcome to stay. Tomorrow night, perhaps?"

O'Connor nodded. "I will see you then."

Gideon shook hands with the priest and departed, feeling full in a way that had nothing to do with the meal. O'Connor was not just an excellent listener but an intelligent conversationalist. He promised to be a pleasant companion, much more so than the incomprehensible Pettifog. What on earth had the man been getting at? There was something deliberate in his remarks, but what?

The mystery occupied Gideon thoroughly. He stopped and heard footsteps stumble to a halt behind him.

"Hello?" Gideon turned. The footpath was empty, the road clear of any traffic. No one there. And yet, he had the distinct impression he wasn't alone…

7

"The contract Mr Westaway signed was clear." Hawarden, the landlord, squared his shoulders. "He rented the house for the quarter, and he paid in full as agreed. There is no room in the agreement for an early cancellation."

Gideon paused in the doorway to the landlord's office. This was not the greeting he was expecting. "I am not here to cancel the lease."

Hawarden blinked. "My secretary told me you're the tenant of 32 Belcairn Road."

"That's right. Gideon Lawes, at your service." Gideon held out his hand.

The landlord stared as if he'd never seen a hand before. "You have moved in, Mr Lawes?"

"Yes. I've been in the house two nights now. Which is why I'm here. The staircase is treacherous. A workman fell." The landlord's office was small, the carpet worn and bare of ornament. That explained why the house was still on his books: Hawarden could not choose his property.

Hawarden stiffened. "I take no responsibility for any accidents that occur. As I told Mr Westaway—"

Gideon forestalled him. "I'd like your permission to make some improvements to the house."

"The house was let as is—" Hawarden paused. "Improvements?"

Gideon nodded. "I wish to widen the staircase and add a light."

The landlord tugged his thin beard. "At Mr Westaway's expense?"

"I must run the improvements by him. On that note, can you recommend a competent carpenter?"

"I believe I can." The landlord's tone was cautious. "You're not asking for the rent back?"

Gideon drew himself up. "I'm not in the habit of telling untruths, Mr Hawarden. I gave my word to Westaway that I would stay in the house and I intend to do so."

"A moment please, Mr Lawes." The landlord stepped out of his office door. A whispered conversation with the secretary followed. Hawarden returned in a much more expansive mood. "I know just the man to make those adjustments. I'll send him round. Anything else you require, Mr Lawes?"

Gideon inclined his head. "I have a question. Who has a key to the house besides myself and Mrs Lightfoot?"

"Assuming that Mr Westaway has had no keys cut, the only other key is our office key, here in my desk."

Gideon frowned. "There is no one else that you know of with access to the house?"

Hawarden raised thin eyebrows. "You've experienced some disturbances, I take it?"

"Disturbances is the right word. My books and papers were thrown about and the furniture toppled." Gideon hesitated to mention the theft. The amount was so paltry, confessing to missing it said more about his financial straits than he wanted.

Hawarden appeared to be on more comfortable ground here. "A sudden gust of wind channelled down the chimney.

You know what these old houses are like. Don't let it get to you, Mr Lawes. The house is well situated and the rent negligible."

Gideon pursed his lips. A gust of wind could not have locked the door.

"While you're here, Mr Lawes, there is a matter I wish to consult you on." Hawarden rested his hands on the desk. "You're the second visitor I've had this morning concerned with number 32 Belcairn Road. An hour ago, a man claiming to be Westaway's representative demanded our key. Without a letter from Mr Westaway allowing it, we cannot in conscience lend the key to anyone, a decision which I am afraid did not please him."

A representative of Westaway? Did he not trust Gideon to do the job? Gideon swallowed, discovering his chest tight. "An older man, with white hair?" Had O'Connor's offer to stay been prearranged?

"No, this was a black-haired man closer to your years."

Gideon recalled feeling watched. "Was the chap's name Pettifog?"

Hawarden snapped his fingers. "It was on the tip of my tongue... You know him, Mr Lawes?"

"Not exactly," Gideon said. "He was asking for a key this morning? I shouldn't give him one, or any information if you can help it."

"He's not Mr Westaway's representative then?"

Gideon spoke coldly. "He is not."

Having concluded his business with the landlord, Gideon returned to the house. "Sudden gust of wind, my foot!" He turned into Belcairn Road. He was no closer to understanding how the thief gained entrance to the house and he had another mystery to boot: Pettifog. What on earth was his interest in the matter? Clearly he intended some mischief... but what?

Gideon stroked his beard. Tempting as it was to blame

Pettifog for the disturbances, he was certain that until the previous night, Pettifog had no idea of the existence of either Gideon or number 32 Belcairn Road. His reaction to Gideon was unfeigned and the timing of his visit to the landlord suggested a hastily concocted plan. Only one thing for it: write to Westaway.

The terrier hurled herself at Gideon, her tail a blur of excitement.

"Steady on," Gideon protested. "I was only out a few hours." Even though he did not intend to encourage demonstrations, he stooped to pat her ears. There was something heartening about being welcomed home, even if it was only by a dog.

When Gideon sat down to pen his letter, the terrier curled on his lap. He did not feel as guilty about this as he should have, reaching down to fondle her silky ears. What would happen to her after Westaway's experiment concluded? Unless he found an occupation, Gideon could not support himself, let alone a pet.

The dog shifted so she could gaze up at him, eyes shining with simple trust.

Write to Westaway, Gideon decided. And then get to work on that treatise. He had to find a job.

The terrier came with him to post the letter. Although the London streets offered plenty of distractions and even a few other dogs, she always returned to Gideon's side.

"Good dog," Gideon told her as she returned from an expedition. He must think of a name...

They paused beside an alleyway, the terrier having discovered a fascinating lamppost. Gideon watched indulgently.

A fragment of conversation caught his ear. "Fine, a sovereign each. But that's my last offer."

Pettifog? Gideon halted. Imagination spurred by Pettifog's visit to the landlord that morning. It couldn't be him...

The voice came from the alley. Gideon peered around the corner.

A slight man in a tailored coat stood with his back to the alley entrance. Gideon had no problem recognising his cologne. Pettifog faced a cluster of grubby children. "You won't get any more from me than that."

"Keep your money." The tallest of the children put her hands on her hips. "You must think we're knobs. Throw stones at number thirty-two?"

Gideon pinched the bridge of his nose. He could feel a headache building.

"This is a simple transaction," Pettifog said acidly. "I wonder that I need to explain it a third time."

"You can explain till you're blue in the face, mister. We ain't doing it. Not one of us is going anywhere near that house, not for all the sovereigns in England." The girl crossed her arms across a scrawny chest as her companions nodded. "That's the Collector's house, that is."

Pettifog scoffed. "And who is this collector you're all so afraid of?"

"He's a nightmare," the girl said. "Only he's real."

"Nightmares aren't real," Pettifog said.

"This one is," said a rumpled boy. "And mean too. Once he's got his sights on someone, that's it. They're done for."

"And what does this nightmare of yours collect? Gullible children?"

"Broken promises," said the girl. "Things you borrowed and didn't return. Unpaid debts. Your life."

Gideon started. That escalated.

His movement must have attracted the children's attention. They looked as one to the girl. "Scarper," she said. "Now."

"Hey!" Pettifog made an ineffectual grab at her as the children darted past. "I'm not done—ow!" A small boy trampled on his boots. "Little brats! Come here and I'll show you what

I think of your collect—" He trailed off, taking in Gideon standing in the entrance to the alley and the dog, barking at the disappearing children. "Nice weather for this time of year, isn't it?"

"I heard you attempting to bribe the children to throw rocks at the house," Gideon said. "I don't know what you're playing at, but it won't work."

"Listen, Lawes." Pettifog stepped towards him. "I admit this doesn't put me in a favourable light, but if you let me explain—"

The terrier growled, her fur bristling. Pettifog came to a halt.

"I agree," Gideon said to the dog. "This has gone far enough. If I see you anywhere near the house, I will report you to the police as a nuisance." He swept down the road.

Adrenalin carried him fast, and Gideon reached the doorstep of 32 Belcairn Road before he'd realised it. He reached for the door handle and it swung open.

Hadn't he locked it before leaving? Was this more of Pettifog's mischief—or the thief returned?

The dog whimpered. She shrunk back from the open door, her ears flat against her skull, her tail tucked down.

"Easy, girl. Stay there." Gideon stepped inside, ears straining for any hint of a presence beside himself.

A floorboard creaked behind him. Before Gideon could turn, a solid object caught him on the back of his head. He fell into darkness.

8

Pain pulsed in his forehead, a dull beat. Gideon lay in a bed, head resting on a pillow, the familiar scent of tallow teasing his nose. Two voices conversed nearby, one light and melodic, the other deeper and curt. The words washed over him, heard but not understood. Neither voice was one Gideon recognised. Where on earth was he? What had happened to him? Why was his head so sore?

"What I mean to say is," the melodic voice whispered, with the air of someone with a point to make, "a man—even if he is behind on the rent—is entitled to walk around his house without falling over prone bodies. It's a gross intrusion, to say nothing of the hazard he poses."

"You'll survive." The deeper voice took his companion's complaint with indifference. "That's a nasty bump on his head. No man would injure himself to stub your toes, Fairweather."

Gideon was aware of a second dull pain, pulsing somewhere around his rib cage. Combined with the ache in his head, his situation was making sense.

"You may have a point there," Fairweather conceded.

"How did he get that bump, anyway? And what's he doing in our house?"

"If I had answers to those questions, don't you think I would have shared them?" The deeper voice had developed a distinct acidic note. "We must wait until our unexpected guest regains consciousness and enlightens us."

"When will that be?"

A heavy sigh. "I do not know. Head injuries—as I told you at least a half hour ago—can be dicey."

"They've never seemed to slow me down much."

"You have a thick skull."

"No need to be like that about it."

The deep-voiced man inhaled. "Would it be too much for you to leave me alone with my patient?"

"And miss the only excitement we've had in months?"

"It's all right," Gideon said. "I'm awake." He opened his eyes.

His first impression was that he was lying in the master bedroom of 32 Belcairn Road. The heavy bedframe was the same, as was the press against the wall. He soon realised his mistake. The flickering candlelight revealed that the bedding was different, paintings hung on the wall, and the bed stand cluttered with shaving paraphernalia, discarded neckwear, novels and an empty bottle. The major point of difference were his companions.

Fairweather could only be the slight man with blonde curls and a waistcoat that was either the height of fashion or of poor taste. He had a round face which, paired with his pout, gave him a childish air. This impression vanished as he blinked, lively interest replacing his dissatisfaction. "About time! If you must collapse in a man's house, introduce your-self first. We didn't know who to send for."

The deep-voiced man was tall, with lank brown hair and a long face. In contrast to his companion's cherubic air, he had the air of a man worn down by responsibilities. He was in his shirt sleeves. "My friend means that, owing to our financial situation, we could not send for a doctor until we had determined that you could cover the costs. Since your pocketbook did not inspire confidence in that direction, you've had to make do with my ministrations."

Gideon spotted his pocketbook sitting on the bed between the two men, his jacket folded over the end of the bed. He struggled into a sitting position. "You went through my pockets."

"Tawdry, I know." Fairweather adopted a soothing tone. "But you were out cold, and we had to do something."

The dark-haired man picked up the pocketbook and held it out. "You will find everything as you left it, Mr Lawes."

Gideon took his pocketbook with a grimace. His head protested the movement with a fresh wave of pain. "You know my name. Might I ask yours?"

"As if you don't know already." Fairweather folded his arms.

"I beg your pardon?" Gideon's head hurt too much for this.

The dark-haired man raised an eyebrow with meaning. "Are you trying to convince us we are unknown to you?"

"I gathered that this is Fairweather." Gideon nodded in his direction—a mistake. His vision swum, and he was silent a long moment, fighting a wave of nausea. "But beyond that, I confess I know nothing of you."

"What were you doing in our house?" Fairweather demanded.

"I thought it was mine. I must have mistaken it in the dark."

Fairweather's frown made his face look petulant—a child robbed of a treat. "That doesn't explain why—"

"Later, I think." The dark-haired man watched Gideon. "Whatever else he is doing, Mr Lawes is not feigning his head injury."

"Certainly not." Bright light interrupted his vision, throbbing in time with his head. "I never lie. My word is my bond."

"Of course." The dark-haired man stood over him, peering at each eye. "Lie still. You're not doing your head any favours."

Gideon found himself settled on his back before he could summon a protest. "I will not stay here so you can insult me."

"You're not leaving," the dark-haired man said. His icy hands pulled the blanket up to Gideon's chin with the detachment of a doctor. "In your current condition, you'll never make it out the room, let alone to the door."

He was right. Gideon shut his eyes, hoping they could not see his defeat.

"Is there anyone we can send for?" the dark-haired man continued.

He could not ask Westaway to rescue him again. "No one."

"Not even Purcock?" Fairweather asked.

Had he fallen on a nail? The pain felt as though it was splitting his skull. "Who?"

Fairweather scoffed. "Who he says. As if he didn't know well—"

"We'll talk about this later," the dark-haired man interrupted. "Mr Lawes needs to rest."

"But Holly—" Fairweather started.

"Mr Lawes will rest better alone." The dark-haired man— Gideon could not think of him as 'Holly'—said. "Out. Find your entertainment elsewhere."

"But we still know nothing!"

"We will learn nothing by forcing a man so ill to speak. We may harm his health by doing so." His doctor draped a cold cloth over Gideon's forehead. "You won't risk his recovery simply to gratify your curiosity?"

"No." The floorboards creaked as Fairweather made his way to the door. "Excuse my most unmannerly behaviour,

Mr Lawes. I wasn't thinking. Holford will take excellent care of you. He's a medical student."

"Was a medical student," Holford said, as Fairweather shut the door behind him. "But Fairweather's right. I'll look after you."

Gideon smiled. "I'm in your debt."

"We'll talk debt later, Mr Lawes." Holford blew out the candle. "Before I let you rest, I have to determine if the blow you received has affected your memory. Your full name?"

"Gideon Lawes."

"Your birthday?"

"June 6th."

"The current year and prime minister?"

"1904 and it's old Balfour." Silence. Gideon opened his eyes. "Something wrong?"

Holford shook his head. "1904. You're sure?"

"Naturally." Gideon rose. "Why…?"

"Do not disturb yourself." Holford laid a firm hand on his shoulder, preventing him from rising. "I was thinking of something else." He hesitated. "What address did you think you were walking into, Mr Lawes?"

"Number thirty-two."

"I see." Holford stood still. His gaze seemed focused, not on Gideon, but on something distant. "Do you have any enemies, Mr Lawes?"

"Enemies?" Gideon started.

"Whoever hit you over the head intended to kill you," Holford said.

A second blow could not have hit him harder. Gideon's ears rang. "Kill me?" he gasped.

"You were not aware then of any threats to your life?"

"You must be mistaken. I can't think of anyone who even knows I'm here, let alone would have a reason to attack me."

"So this is not your usual neighbourhood? Are you in hiding, Mr Lawes?"

Gideon's head pulsed. "No. I can think of no one with a grudge against me." Except perhaps Barchester Junior. Barchester Senior hadn't been too pleased with him either… His breath caught. Not Pettifog?

"Ah," Holford said, making Gideon start. He'd forgotten how close the man stood. "So there is someone."

"The idea is ludicrous," Gideon protested, but his voice lacked conviction. "What you suggest—well, I might have died."

"Yes," Holford said, his mouth twisting. "I rather think that was the point."

9

Gideon's head no longer hurt, so long as he did nothing strenuous—like sitting up, rolling over or breathing too deeply. He lay still, listening to the sounds of the street outside. Belcairn Road could never be called busy, but today everything seemed muffled in thick silence.

Fog, Gideon thought, and regretted it. Even thinking hurt.

The door rattled. After a few false attempts, the handle turned. Fairweather stepped inside with a self-congratulatory expression and a tray bearing a pot of tea, cups, and a mostly empty bottle of whiskey. "Didn't drop a thing."

He seemed to expect a response. "Well done?"

"Holly said you wouldn't be hungry, but that you might drink a cup of tea." Fairweather halted as he reached the bedside and realised he had nowhere to place his tray. "Can you sit up?"

"I can try." Gideon eased himself up.

Fairweather set the tray on the bed. "Holly said you'd be feeling rotten, and that I'm not allowed to pester you with questions. Even if you haven't told us what you're doing here or why you were lying in our hallway ready to trip unsuspecting passers-by."

Gideon watched him pour a cup of tea and drop a cube of sugar in it. "Aren't you going to ask me if I want sugar?"

"Holly said you would need the extra sustenance." Fairweather considered the teacup. "Or would you prefer a drop of spirit?"

Gideon looked up from the adulterated teacup with horror. "Now you're asking?"

Fairweather shrugged, adding a dash of the whiskey to the tea. "You don't know what a rarity this is. Holly's been pretending we didn't have a drop in the house for months. I should have known he was holding out. For medicinal use only, he says. Ha!" Fairweather added a generous splash of whiskey to his own cup. "It seems a shame to dilute this considering how long it will be before we see it again."

Gideon sipped his tea. It was not the affront he was expecting. "Are you sure you should speak so plain? I am a stranger."

"Not that much of a stranger," Fairweather countered. "You're sleeping in my bed."

Gideon looked down at his sheets with some dismay. "I beg your pardon."

"Anyway, I don't see the point in hiding it. You have eyes. You're bound to notice that we're in dire straits. Better to be honest about it."

"An admirable philosophy." Gideon scratched his chin. "Hard times then?"

"Dickens himself couldn't write harder." Fairweather emptied the rest of the whiskey into his cup. "It's not enough that we moved to the most out of the way part of London, but we can't even leave the house for fear of seeing someone we know. We must owe money to half the city."

Gideon smiled, despite his better instincts. "I hadn't

needed to borrow yet, but I was almost down to my last penny."

"You mean you're not a collector? Then what are you doing here—no, don't tell me. Holly made me promise." Fairweather pouted. "I don't care if he was a medical student, he's got no right to act as though he's so superior." He looked at Gideon. "You're not a medical student, are you? Past or present?"

"No." Gideon hesitated. In his present situation, his glory days at Oxford were cause for embarrassment rather than celebration, but there was something in Fairweather's artless confidences that demanded reciprocity. "I was a Balliol man."

Fairweather brightened. "They threw me out of Magdalen."

Why on earth did he sound so pleased about that? "Oh?"

"Bringing the college into disrepute. Splendid times. Until Father got into a huff and cut off my allowance." His expression grew brooding. "As if he didn't do the same thing as an undergraduate. Then again, I suppose that is the thing fathers do. What about you?" He sized Gideon up. "I don't remember seeing you about the place."

"I devoted myself to my studies." Gideon grimaced. "Rather a swot, I'm afraid."

"I suppose you didn't know any better," Fairweather said. "And you'll be company for Holly. You can have intellectual conversations or whatever it is chaps like you do."

Gideon's mouth twitched. "Holly didn't strike me as suffering from lack of conversation."

"You don't know him as I do." Fairweather leaned back, holding his teacup with an almost proprietary air. "I'm ignorant on science, religion and law, but I know Holly. Between us, you picked the best imaginable time to get knocked over the head. No, I don't mean it like that. I'm sure it's inconvenient for you to say nothing of the pain…" Fairweather trailed to a halt. "This is why Holly needs someone to have sensible conversations with."

Gideon's mouth curved. "Matter of fact, the pain's not as bad as it was. I haven't noticed it at all while you've been talking."

"You're feeling better? That's good. Though you mustn't get better too soon." Fairweather leaned forward. "Not being able to go out and see people, not having visitors... It wears on a chap. Holly doesn't like to admit it, but he's feeling it."

It was one thing to accept Fairweather's confidences, quite another to listen to Holford's. The former medical student gave the impression of being more circumspect with his history than his companion. "Mr Holford strikes me as capable of taking care of himself."

"That's just the impression he gives," Fairweather said. "The change in him would shock you."

"I don't think—"

"He always had foul moods. But his sulks now last for days. Even weeks... And sometimes—" Fairweather caught himself. "But I shouldn't be telling you this. Holly hates being talked about."

Gideon grimaced. "I tried to stop you."

"You shouldn't be so easy to talk to." Fairweather pulled a face at him. "You must be in demand at parties."

Gideon swallowed. "I don't go to a lot of parties."

"You astound me. Well, you must be the popular member of the family then."

Gideon attempted jovial. "Matter of fact, I live alone."

Fairweather squinted at him. "No family?"

So much for jovial. "I'm an orphan. My uncle raised me and sent me to school, but no more. He was too busy with his parish to have time for a nephew."

Fairweather considered him. "But you've got friends."

Gideon winced. "Let's just say that you are not the only one in disgrace."

"No!" Fairweather beamed. "I didn't think you had it in you! Let's drink to that." He somehow wrung a few more drops out of the whiskey bottle. "To disgrace!"

"Well now," Gideon protested. "If we drink to something, we should make it something worthwhile."

"True—there's been rather too much disgrace around here," Fairweather agreed. "How about new friends?" He gave Gideon a glowing smile.

Something fluttered in the vicinity of Gideon's lungs. He nodded. "To friends." They tapped teacups.

"Splendid. Now that we're chums, what landed you on disgrace street?" Fairweather resettled himself. "As long as it won't hurt your head to answer."

"It hurts my pride more than anything." As Gideon spoke, the bedroom door handle turned, the door swinging inward. Gideon turned towards it. "Everyone else seems to think the outcome obvious, but I never saw..." He trailed off. The doorway was empty. "I thought—" What had he thought?

"Old house," Fairweather blurted. "Uneven floorboards, warped doorframes. You know the type. Always popping open."

Gideon narrowed his eyes. "Warped doorframe doesn't explain the turning handle. I saw it."

Fairweather scoffed. "You must have imagined it." He was pale. The hand that held his cup trembled.

"I never imagine," Gideon said. "I've been told I'm deficient in the imaginative organs. What opened the door?"

"The third member of the household." Fairweather pressed his lips together. "Unlike you, this guest is unwelcome and unexpected."

"A guest?" Gideon's skin tingled. He could almost feel the pressure in the air.

Fairweather downed his remaining whiskey in one gulp and stood. He closed the door. "He's harmless, so long as you're not standing in a doorway when he's coming or going.

Keeps decent hours, on the whole. Banging doors and opening curtains seem to be his entire stock in trade. With a bit of effort, it's possible to imagine he's just a breeze. And he keeps the rent down, so he's more beneficial than anything."

Gideon sank back against the pillows. His head was pounding again, fit to explore. "You're not telling me this house is haunted, too?"

Fairweather stared at him. "Too? Lawes, you are a dark horse. Here I was trying not to frighten you."

Gideon set his teacup aside, ignoring the protest building in his forehead. "Tell me everything."

10

G hosts were the product of ignorance and imagination, nothing more. Gideon rolled over, unable to settle. His head throbbed, a steady ache. The blankets stuck to him. He couldn't rid his mind of the image of the door handle, moving under an invisible hand...

Tricks. Holford and Fairweather didn't want company. It was in their interest to drive him away. A ghost would encourage him not to linger.

There were easier ways to get rid of him. Fairweather's appeal for his company felt genuine. He wanted to be friends. Or was Gideon's desire for friendship clouding his judgement?

If only he could think! Gideon rolled onto his back. Taking a deep breath, he took mental hold of himself. He would lie still and clear his mind. He could rest and recover his strength until sleep claimed him.

The throbbing in his head persisted. Gideon listened to the sounds coming from the next room. He could not discern words, but he could distinguish the light music of Fairweather's voice interspersed with the occasional rumble from Holford. It took some time for the pair to settle, judging from the squeaking bedsprings. At length, they fell silent.

The ache in his head had dulled enough that sleep encroached. Gideon's mind drifted. He was too tired for thought. Impressions washed over him. Some time later, he noticed an unfamiliar noise.

A wooden tap, followed by a sweeping sound—or was that something dragging? Gideon listened without curiosity. His senses were dulled, exhausted like his body and his mind. How long had he heard the sound before he'd noticed it? The wooden tap was almost at the door.

The dog. Gideon remembered the terrier was at number 32. Mrs Lightfoot would have noticed his absence and fed the dog. Complaining all the while about her joints, no doubt…

A faint light flickered beneath the door frame, as if someone stood outside with a candle in hand.

His heart thudded. At least that organ still had impetus! Gideon had a moment's premonition. The door handle turned, the catch clicking as the door swung open.

The tapping returned, along with the dragging sound. Candlelight accompanied them.

Acting on some buried instinct, Gideon lay still. He concentrated on keeping his breathing even. When he was confident he'd mastered himself, he opened his eyes the merest crack.

The man regarding him was a stranger. His skin was pale and his overlong hair, a relic of a former age, hung around hollow cheeks. He wore a faded looking robe over his clothes, and he leaned on a gnarled walking stick. As the man took a heavy step towards him, Gideon guessed the dragging sound was slippers rubbing against wooden floorboards. Gideon screwed his eyes shut and lay still. Beneath the blankets, he dug his hands into the mattress. To divulge awareness of the man's presence would be fatal.

The man paused by the bedside; the candle raised.

Did he see Gideon? His throat was sore, his lips parched. He did not dare wet them. All the air was sucked from the room, leaving a void containing only himself and the awful, silent man.

He would scream. Gideon's mind raced, searching for some way to stave off this disaster. None came to mind. He would scream and the man would be upon him in an instant.

The walking stick rattled once, the shuffling resumed. The candlelight dimmed and then evened out again. The pressure eased. Gideon squinted between closed lids.

The man had turned aside, revealing that grey streaked his brown hair. An old man. He held the candle in one hand, while the other opened the wardrobe.

Searching the room? The man shuffled around the room, peering into every shadow and opening every drawer. A gleam of repressed excitement shone in his eyes. A lunatic? The light of his candle cast a mean light on the room, disclosing empty walls and peeling wallpaper.

Something about the wallpaper tugged at Gideon's memory. Before he could put his finger on it, the man paused. Whatever he sought, he had not found it. The only thing in the room the man had not searched was the bed.

Gideon's breath hitched. Anything but that. Lying still while that man rummaged through the bed sheets or—even worse—laid his skeletal hands on him was beyond endurance. He flinched. The man's stick, left propped against the bed, toppled to the floor.

The man whirled around, too fast for Gideon to feign unconsciousness. He stepped forward, moving with a speed that his age belied.

"Stay back." Gideon's head collided with the headboard as he pulled himself back. "Don't come near me!"

Bright lights danced before his eyes, filling his vision. Splitting pain made his eyes water and sent a wave of nausea through him. Consciousness ebbed from him, even as cold fingers settled on his arm. He made a feeble attempt to shake himself free. "Unhand me!"

The effort was useless, the hands closing around his arm. Darkness stole over him. Gideon surrendered without another thought. Faced with the terror of the old man, unconsciousness was a blessed relief.

11

"Do not think this any reflection on your hospitality, but I cannot—I cannot—spend another moment in this room." What little daylight made it into Belcairn Road filtered through the bedroom window, falling on the familiar shapes of Fairweather's clutter. The sight of the homely bits and pieces did nothing to dispel the impression Gideon's ghastly visitor had left behind him. "If you'd seen him yourself, you'd understand. I—the dreadful cunning in his eyes, the menace..." Gideon shuddered. Even after waking and assuring himself he was alone, the atmosphere of nightmare persisted.

Holford gripped Gideon's wrist. He pursed his lips. "Your pulse is fast, bordering on erratic. Whatever you saw last night upset you."

"I saw a man, just like I've been telling you," Gideon snapped.

Fairweather perched on the end of the bed, watching him with an awed expression. "Fancy seeing the ghost! We've been here months now, and he hasn't shown himself to us once."

"We don't know this was the ghost." The shadows under

Holford's eyes were more pronounced in daylight. He released Gideon's wrist and leaned in, holding a stethoscope to Gideon's chest. "Breathe."

"What else could it be? The description, his presence in this room—" Fairweather's excitement was feverish, too strong to be contained in the bedroom.

"Whoever he was," Gideon said, "I am not staying here. I must leave." The last words were almost a whisper, his strength failing him.

"The sofa in the morning room could make a tolerable daybed," Holford said. "Suppose you take a few pillows downstairs and see what you can do, Fairweather?"

Gideon breathed out, shutting his eyes in relief.

Fairweather bundled up the pillows. "Shan't be long."

"Open your eyes." Holford squinted at each eye. "No serious harm done. You'll be fine, so long as you take it easy."

"Are you—" Gideon paused. 'Sure I'm not mad?' seemed too direct, but how else to phrase his fear?

"Qualified?" Holford's smile was mocking. "I made it all the way through my degree and was in the final stages of qualification before being turfed out. Even if I don't have the degree to prove it, I know my stuff." His words had a bite.

Gideon raised his hands. "I wasn't—that is—" The last thing he wanted to do was offend anyone and once again, he'd blundered straight into it!

"In case you're worried that I mixed up my medicines or killed a patient, you can set your mind at rest. I was observed in a compromising situation with a patient and summarily dismissed." Holford's mouth twisted. "That the patient was an active party in the compromising meant nothing to the Board. All those years of hard work, my tuition fees, my future—gone."

Gideon felt an answering weight in his chest. "There's nothing you can do?"

"Not much call for former medical students. The small

inheritance I got from my parents all went towards my tuition. I've got no way of setting myself up in a new trade. I subsist on Fairweather's generosity and those of the neighbourhood who can't afford treatment by a qualified doctor."

"When Father dies and I inherit the estate, the first thing I'm doing is installing you as steward." Fairweather had returned. "You can doctor the tenants to your heart's content."

"Treating country bumpkins for nothing. Just what I always dreamed of." Holford unwound his stethoscope and dropped it back into his bag.

"Don't be like that." Fairweather elbowed Holford. "I want Lawes to like us."

"That's very much your department," Holford returned. "Help me get him downstairs and I'll leave you to it." He turned to Gideon. "Think you can stand?"

Gideon wasn't sure, but he could not endure another moment in the bedroom. "Only one way to find out."

Holford gripped one arm. "Fairweather, take his other side."

"I have done this before, you know." Fairweather wrapped an arm around Gideon. "Ready, Lawes? Easy does it."

Gideon's head swum and his knees sagged. He leaned on the two men either side of him.

"Steady." Holford watched him, his habitual distance replaced by concern. He would have made a good doctor. "If standing's too much, we can carry you."

That was an indignity Gideon would not bear. "I can manage." He swallowed and took a careful step forward.

"That's the way." Fairweather's tone was light. "This takes me back. Just like heading home after a night out on the town."

Carefully, they navigated the stairs and the downstairs. Gideon tried to keep his eyes closed—the nausea was less when he couldn't see—but the similarity of the entrance to

that of number 32 struck him. This impression was rein-
forced by the discovery that Fairweather and Holford's
morning room was identical in structure to his study.

"There." The sofa had seen better days, but Fairweather
had made it hospitable, draping a blanket over it and fluffing
the pillows. He installed Gideon on it with care. "Are you
comfortable?"

Comfortable wasn't the word, but anything was better
than the bedroom. "Quite. You know it's remarkable, just
how this house resembles mine. I'm no longer surprised I
mistook them in the dark."

"There's no mystery there." Holford stepped back,
surveying Gideon. "These old houses were all built at the
same time by the same builder. A nice little nest egg. He
could collect the rents and, when he needed a little more, sell
off one of them."

"That makes sense." Gideon's nose twitched. The sour
smell of cheap tobacco hung in the air.

"You're to take it easy for the next few hours," Holford
instructed. "No moving. Not even talking, if you can help it.
Moving downstairs took a lot out of you."

Gideon thought better of nodding. "I'll take my medicine.
Thank you, Holford."

"Fairweather, you're not to pester him. Lawes, being in a
new room might wake memories of your accident. Avoid
thinking about it. You're still healing from the shock you
received. Unnecessary agitation at this stage could lead to a
serious setback." Holford gave them both a stern look and
walked out of the room.

"Allow me." Fairweather drew the blanket up over
Gideon.

Gideon settled himself against the pillows. "Holford
smokes tobacco, doesn't he?"

"I make him take his pipe outside. I was consumptive as a

child. The smoke of a pipe, especially that awful concoction Holly uses, sets me off in a coughing fit."

Gideon nodded. He'd solved the mystery of the smoke he'd smelled in the courtyard. Holford was the culprit. Their houses must be close, perhaps next door to each other.

Fairweather tilted his head. "Are you missing your pipe?"

"No, I never gained the habit." It was a luxury that Gideon denied himself. "Just wondering."

There was a desk in the corner, very close to where Gideon had placed his writing desk. Fairweather turned the chair around to face Gideon and sat. "I know Holly said you should rest, but I don't feel easy leaving you alone, not after the fright you had last night."

"The least said about that the better." Already the change in environment coupled with the light was improving Gideon's nerves. "I'll be fine."

"All the same, unless you think I'll stop you resting, I might keep you company." Fairweather pulled a face. "I've got to work on my accounts."

Gideon felt himself pleased, though he was hard pressed to put his finger on the cause. "By all means."

Fairweather smiled and took a record book from the desk. When he opened it, a few scraps of paper escaped. He set those to one side, and, taking up a lead pencil with a sigh, set to his task.

Gideon let his eyes drift closed. He had not passed a restful night at all. Even before the dreadful old man had made his appearance, his thoughts had pursued themselves in exhaustive circles. The moment he was still, tiredness settled over him like a blanket.

Was this tiredness? A strange warm feeling in his chest counteracted the weight of his body and the dullness of his thoughts. Content? Gideon felt pleased with himself after completing a piece of work to his satisfaction, but he could not be congratulating himself for walking downstairs with help.

One of Fairweather's scraps of paper escaped him. As he knelt to retrieve it, his elbow caught the desk, sending his pencil rolling to the floor. He cursed in a whisper, mindful of Gideon even in his moment of temper.

Gideon's mouth twitched, the corners forcing their way upwards into a smile. Was that it? He had always considered himself a man of solitary habits, but he could not deny that there was something very restful about Fairweather's presence, and his quiet regard. Perhaps…

On that half-formed hope, Gideon fell asleep.

12

"Blast, drat and confound it all!" A chair scraped along the floor.

Gideon jerked awake. Had the ghastly intruder returned?

A quick look revealed that he still lay on the sofa in the morning room. Fairweather knelt, scanning the floor for something he didn't find. He moved on the armchairs, feeling down the backs of the chairs.

"Lost something?" Gideon heaved himself into a sitting position.

"Did I wake you?" Fairweather's dismay sounded genuine. "Sorry, old chap. I didn't even think."

Gideon rubbed his eyes. "No harm done. What are you looking for?"

Fairweather ran a hand through his hair. "Just making sure I had overlooked nothing. I'm short—again."

It took Gideon a moment to parse Fairweather's words. "You're searching the chair cushions on the chance you've overlooked a few pence."

Fairweather's mouth drooped. "When you put it like that, it sounds pitiful… But you never know. I found a sovereign I must have put away for safekeeping in a drawer once. Since then—well, I know it's hopeless, but I still have to check. It's a compulsion, almost—and every little bit helps."

Just how bad were his finances? "No need to say more. I know what it's like to count every penny."

Fairweather nodded. "That's it, isn't it? There's something so sordid about pennies… A gentleman shouldn't have to mind them, so I don't. But then, my affairs always come out so muddled. No matter what I do, I always end up owing someone—and debt isn't gentlemanly either."

Gideon nodded towards the record book on the desk. "I'm not bad with figures. Would you like me to look?"

Fairweather glanced at his record book, his brow furrowing. "I don't know. A chap's account book is personal."

"I've slept in your bed," Gideon pointed out. "How much more personal can you get? Besides," he looked down. Why were words so hard? "You and Holford, you've done so much for me, and I just blundered into your house uninvited. I'm not an engaging fellow or someone you'd choose to have around—"

"Steady on!" Fairweather protested. "You've not been a hardship you know, and your company—"

Gideon held up a hand. "Please. Let me finish." He took a deep breath. "I'm not good with words. Or people, or much of anything except sums. If I can be of any use to you, I would like to be—if only to thank you for your kindness."

Fairweather placed a hand on Gideon's shoulder. "It's not kindness when it gives me pleasure, but if it means that much to you, wrestle with my accounts to your heart's content. Only you must promise not to judge me. Subtraction was never my strong point. Addition either, come to think of it."

Strange. A hand was just a hand, but Fairweather's hand plus Gideon's shoulder added up to something more than mere touch. "I shall keep my thoughts on your mathematics to myself."

"Appreciated." Fairweather scooped up his record book and held it out to Gideon. "Here it is. I wish you joy of it. It's given me none."

Gideon opened the record book to a sense of recognition. The leger with its smudged ink, the sums in the margins and the scraps of paper was not familiar, but there was a comfort in the familiarity. More than that: recognition. "It was your paper I found."

Fairweather pulled him up to sit on the desk. "Oh?"

Gideon pulled his pocketbook out of the breast pocket of his jacket. He found the scrap of paper folded away within. "I picked this up. I'm afraid I made some corrections."

Fairweather glanced down at the paper. "Holford and I were astonished to see my receipt in your wallet."

Gideon leaned back against the sofa. "That's why you thought I was a debt collector."

Fairweather shrugged. "It was a rum coincidence. You stumbling into our house and having my paper on you."

"Not so rum. We're neighbours. If we live close enough I can smell Holford's pipe, then we're close enough a stray paper could drift into my house." Gideon looked over the leger. "Pass me that pen."

Fairweather kept his accounts with a carelessness of someone who'd never worried about pennies. His figures wandered between the columns allotted for income and expenses, and the notes beside them were often indecipherable, even to their author. Making sense of the jumble took all of Gideon's attention. While he worked, Fairweather kept up a steady commentary.

"I economise where I can… But a man has to have standards, you know. I'm a Fairweather. I have to look presentable."

"You'll be the best dressed chap in the debtors' prison. Assuming they don't repossess your wardrobe."

Holford's entrance had the effect of the curtains thrown

open at the start of the day. Gideon blinked, roused from his sums. "It's not that bad."

"You've got a task Sisyphus himself wouldn't envy." Holford set down a package and knelt before the fire. "If you've got any sense, you'll give it up now. They're Fairweather's expenses. Let him wrestle with them."

"Now, Holly. Lawes is doing me a very kind favour. You mustn't—" He paused, peering at the package. "Sausages?"

"That's right."

"I thought the butcher said he would no longer accept credit until we settled our bill."

Holford didn't look up. "He did."

"So what changed his mind? Or did you find a different butcher?"

"You'll be happier not knowing."

Fairweather frowned at him. "I will not stand for anything underhanded."

"If you must know, some daft housewife gave the butcher the wrong address. By the time she realises her mistake, the sausages will spoil. We can't let them go to waste, can we?" Holford settled back on his heels, reaching for a toasting fork.

"I suppose… But they're still not our sausages."

"Take that up with the housewife once she realises her mistake. In the meantime, I'm starving. No matter what you do, I will eat."

Fairweather's gaze lingered on the sausages. He shook himself, turning to Gideon. "Lawes, you don't think we should take advantage of some poor woman's mistake, do you? I mean, for all we know she's got a family to feed. And it's not as if we're in any position to pay her back."

"Tell you what," Gideon said. "There're some sausages in the icebox at my place. When the housewife realises her mistake, we can offer her those."

Holford glanced up. "How very fortunate."

"But then we're taking your sausages," Fairweather protested, but there was less strength in the protest.

"I insist," Gideon said. "You've done so much for me. And I have to admit, I'm hungry too." He did not remember the last time he'd eaten. Until the sausages appeared, he had not even noticed an appetite. Now he was famished.

Fairweather's smile was fervent. "We'll pay you back."

"That will be the day," Holford remarked, adding a third sausage to his toasting fork.

"I will. No matter how long it takes." Fairweather drew himself up. "A Fairweather always settles his debts. It's our family motto."

"Perhaps if you didn't have so many debts, your family wouldn't need it as a motto."

Fairweather elbowed Holford, crouching next to him to watch the sausages being toasted. "Our motto is more than just money, you know. It's about honour, fulfilling the obligations of the Fairweather name."

"You come from an estate then?" Gideon asked.

"Yes. An old one too. Dates back to the dissolution of the monasteries. Fairweathers fought for the crown in every major battle since. With that history behind us, we've got to think of our honour."

"I always assumed that honour was more integral to a man who lacked everything else," Gideon said. "Myself for example. All my life, I've known I must support myself, and I cannot look to family and have too much pride to accept charity from friends. All I have is my integrity. My honour is my word. I've never lied and if I say I will do something, I do it."

Fairweather looked up, his eyes shining. "I knew you'd understand, Lawes! We—"

"Idealists the both of you," Holford said. "You're living in the real world—a world where honour is not the currency you think it is."

Fairweather scoffed. "I suppose the only important thing is money?"

"By no means. Money is a means to an end." Holford withdrew the toasting fork from the fire, inspecting his work. "Money is power, and power's the only thing worth having."

"Oh, come now. The only thing?" Fairweather's tone was gentle.

Holford raised an eyebrow at him. "At the moment, a well-cooked sausage ranks high in my priorities." He used a fork to slide the cooked sausages off the toasting fork and onto a waiting plate. "Well, Lawes as our guest and benefactor, you take the first one."

Gideon dragged his thoughts away from trying to decipher Fairweather's tone. "That's very kind." The polite thing would have been to insist that his hosts help themselves first, but the smell of the sausage drove that—and all other—thoughts from his head. It was hard to be honourable on an empty stomach.

13

No sausages had ever tasted better or been consumed with more gusto. Gideon felt better than he had in days.

His companions shared his exhilaration, Fairweather in party spirits, Holford unbending so far as to smile once or twice, and even make a sardonic observation that, coming from anyone else, he'd have termed a joke. Gideon felt satisfied in a way that had nothing to do with his full stomach. He'd satiated a hunger whose existence he'd never even suspected, and he felt content all the way to his bones. And from what? Fairweather attempting to make him the referee in his current argument with Holford, and the ironic glances that Holford gave him when scoring a point off Fairweather. He'd not felt companionship like this since his college days.

Thinking of college brought Westaway to mind. Gideon stroked his chin, remembering the second bedroom. Was this companionship what Westaway had alluded to? How had he known what Gideon hadn't known himself?

Holford stretched out in his armchair. "I should call it a night, but I'm dashed unwilling. There's something about a fire."

"Very lucky you finding that coal in the cellar," Fairweather said. "Not to mention that bottle of Madeira." It had been drunk in no short order, and its effects no doubt contributed to their joint sense of wellbeing.

Holford glanced at Gideon. "Lucky is the word."

Fairweather stretched, climbing out of his armchair. "The night wants just one thing to make it prefect." He trailed his fingers along Holford's cheek, then leaned in, pressing his mouth to Holford's.

Gideon jerked in surprise, his mouth falling open. This was indecent—improper—whatever it was. A kiss? But—

Holford thrust Fairweather back. "Have you learned nothing, you little idiot? Lawes—"

"It's all right," Fairweather said with his usual assurance. "Lawes is one of ours. Aren't you?" He looked to Gideon with such implicit confidence.

Gideon was equal parts flattered and confused. "I don't quite follow your meaning."

Fairweather's mouth fell open. "But you don't object to my company. And you've looked at my account books—"

"The most intimate transaction that could ever take place between two men." Holford covered his face with hands.

"You've never attempted to kiss me," Gideon pointed out.

"And if I did? Does the thought—it doesn't repulse you, does it?" An expression of anxiety replaced Fairweather's usually sunny expression.

Gideon had never imagined being kissed by Fairweather. He gave it his full consideration. "I don't seem to have any strong feelings either way. On the whole it might be pleasant, but I'm not sure it would be appropriate. If I interpret the situation correctly—" And why had there not been a paper on this at Oxford? "You appear to have a prior understanding with Holford."

Fairweather beamed. "A prior understanding. I like that."

"A prior understanding and a present headache." Holford massaged his temples. "Well, I don't suppose it matters now."

Fairweather pouted. "What do you mean, 'now'?"

Gideon raised a hand. "A question, if I may. Your relationship—I take it your understanding extends beyond friendship?"

Fairweather beamed. "It certainly does."

"Are there other men who have…understandings…of this nature?"

Fairweather cast a look at Holford. "Not everyone takes this so well. People can be very judgmental."

"Ha!" Holford reached for the bottle of madeira.

Gideon concentrated on his train of thought. "How would one tell if he was… 'one of yours?'"

Fairweather sat on the arm of Gideon's sofa. "Ever been distracted by the thought of someone? You recite every word they've said to you in your mind, you walk by their medical practice hoping to see them in the window, you spend your waking hours thinking of excuses to meet with them, and the merest accidental touch from them sets your skin on fire."

Gideon considered. "I can't say that I have."

"Has anyone ever so annoyed you that dismissing them from your mind is impossible? You act in ways irreconcilable with common sense, and yet, you cannot stop yourself," Holford added.

Gideon caught his breath. His undergraduate years came into sharp focus, as if he'd found the right telescopic lens with which to view it. "Westaway."

"Westaway?" Fairweather looked as alert as the terrier upon hearing the kitchen cupboard open. "A friend?"

"My rival at Balliol." Gideon had always been a serious scholar, but his desire to beat Westaway to the first had surprised even him. The knowledge that after every exam, Westaway was also looking at his results had added weight to his achievements, and, while sneering at his rival's affectations, he'd paid careful attention to everything Westaway did. No wonder his first had seemed so flat. He'd got the prize, the envied position at Barchester's bank, but without Westaway, there was no meaning in his achievement.

"Do you still keep in touch?" Fairweather asked.

He hesitated. "Not usually, but I ran into him last week. It's because of him I'm in Belcairn Road at all."

Fairweather leaned in. "And what does Westaway think of you?"

"Who on earth knows? He's not a man so much as an enigma." Albeit an enigma with a taste for the finer things in life. "But no, that can't be it. There's not the physical reaction you describe." And while Gideon had the utmost respect for Westaway's mind, he could not imagine kissing him, ever.

"Not everyone goes for the physical side of things. There's those that go in for the Platonic ideal." Fairweather attempted to look wise. "Others who find everything they need in friendships. 'Confirmed bachelor' can mean a lot of things—"

"Can it also extend to inserting yourself into the affairs of complete strangers, asking impertinent questions and acting with childishness scarcely to be believed in a grown man?"

Holford chuckled. "Is that a stab at Fairweather?"

Gideon choked. "No, not at all! I—"

"Lawes has someone else in mind." Fairweather said with measured dignity. "You'd better watch yourself, Holly, or you'll find yourself a confirmed bachelor." He turned back to Gideon. "Who is this chap?"

Gideon hesitated, but if Pettifog had gone to the lengths of following him from the club, he might nose around the rest of Belcairn Road. "His name's Pettifog. The most intolerable bounder I've ever met." He recounted their meeting. "I could be mistaken. But for him to take a complete dislike to me because I sat at Westaway's table and have undertaken a job for him seems, in the light of what you've just told me, connected."

"Jealous," pronounced Fairweather. "And I should know. Holly, believe it or not, used to get very sour if I so much as smiled at someone. He would have no issues inserting himself into a landlord's office on the flimsiest of pretences, would you, Holly?"

Holly snorted, standing up. "Those days are gone. I am, I hope, a much wiser man." He nodded to Gideon. "I'm going to retire now. If Fairweather foists any more unasked for confidences upon you, send him away. Doctor's orders. You need to rest."

"I was just about to retire myself." Fairweather slid off the end of the sofa. "You'll be all right here, Lawes?"

"Perfectly." The pleasant evening they'd shared could not erase the memory of the creeping man from his mind. "I shall be more than comfortable here."

Holford quit the room, but Fairweather lingered. "It feels mean making you sleep down here when there is a perfectly suitable bed lying empty upstairs."

"Only one bed?" Considering the evening's conversation, Holford and Fairweather's sleeping arrangements took on a new connotation. Gideon's cheeks heated, and he dropped Fairweather's gaze. "I am sorry. It's none of my business."

"The apology should be on my end. I assumed a lot—much more than was appropriate. I'm glad you took it in stride." Fairweather grimaced. "What I'm trying to say is that I like you and, well, I'm glad, is all."

It was not the warmest praise Gideon had ever received, or even the most grammatical, but it was pleasing regardless. "Your understanding with Holford—does it make you happy?"

"Very." Fairweather's face lit up. "He's the only thing that could make this—the loneliness and the scrounging and all of it—bearable. If I didn't have him… Well, I've just got to make this up to him." He gave Gideon a cheerful grimace and followed Holford out of the room.

Gideon stretched out on the sofa. He drew the blanket up although the room, still lit by the fire, wasn't cold. Come to think of it, even without the fire, he hadn't noticed it being chilly.

The genuine nature of Holford and Fairweather's relationship was a revelation, not to mention Pettifog or his own fascination with Westaway. He had so much to ponder that it would be a surprise if he slept at all.

14

The scrape of shifting furniture was replacing the sound of market carts in the street as the signal to wake. Gideon stretched, his feet encountering the far end of the sofa. He opened his eyes.

Fairweather was on his knees in front of his desk. He had pulled the bookcase out from the wall to check behind it and was now continuing his search by emptying the drawers one by one.

"Any luck?"

Fairweather grimaced. "None. And yet, there's got to be something I've overlooked."

Gideon heaved his legs over the edge of the sofa. "Something since yesterday?"

Fairweather pushed the drawer he was checking closed. "I know this is unreasonable. And yet I cannot help it. I keep asking myself if I've checked everywhere, if there might not be something…" He turned to the last drawer, spilling its contents across the floor.

This was not the affable man who had teased and joked the night before. As Gideon watched, he emptied a drawer for a second time. "Is everything…" All right was the wrong word. "Is there something you haven't told me?"

Fairweather paused. "I can't explain it. There's this feeling I get sometimes, a premonition. That something bad will happen, and when it does… Well, I want to know that my affairs are in order." His shoulders drooped, and he offered Gideon a rueful smile. "When I say it out loud, it sounds farfetched."

"A bit," Gideon agreed. "But knowing what I do about how seriously you take the family motto, I can understand why."

"That's just it," Fairweather said. "I've got this creeping suspicion that I will die, my obligations unfulfilled."

Gideon felt a stab of alarm. "You're not unwell?"

Fairweather started shoving the drawers back into the desk. "I could be better fed, but I'm healthy. Irritatingly so, Holford says. Rotten chest aside, I have a robust constitution."

"So then…?"

"I had a nasty fall a few weeks ago," Fairweather said. "I was in my cups, mistook a stair. Ended up in a heap at the bottom. Holly says it's a wonder I didn't break my neck. I suppose that is behind this. No man likes a reminder of his mortality."

"I can relate." The memory of Gideon's own accident brought up a twinge of pain. "Let me get back to work on your accounts."

It was a pleasant way to pass a day, Fairweather pottering around the study, putting the mess he'd made back to rights, Gideon finding substantial satisfaction in taming his unruly figures. They didn't talk much, but it was companionable all the same.

So companionable, that it took Gideon a while to realise that something was wrong. As he reached the end of Fairweather's accounts, unease prodded him. He rested his hands on the report book, trying to identify the source of his concern.

"That bad?"

Fairweather's question made him start. "Sorry, I was lost in thought."

"You looked it." Fairweather ran a hand through his blond curls. "How much am I done for?"

Gideon hesitated. "I'm not sure. Some of your numbers don't look right." There were amounts that didn't match their corresponding receipts and what looked like duplicates. "Is there anything I can check these against?"

"They're in that much of a muddle?" Fairweather glanced upstairs. "Holly's got his own set of accounts. I'll see if I can find them."

"Please." Gideon nodded. His chest was tight, his palms sweaty. He had the awful feeling… "No." Once was enough. Or maybe his experience at Barchesters had left him paranoid, and he was seeing things that weren't there…

The wait for Fairweather to return was intolerable. Gideon got up from the sofa, walking the length of the room. He couldn't settle. The need to have an answer worried at him. He had to know if his suspicions were founded.

"Here they are." Fairweather returned. "Holly was still fast asleep. It's been a while since he's let himself go. Like I said, you're excellent company."

Gideon forced a smile, accepting the book. "I hope you don't mind if I work on this alone? I'd like to concentrate."

Fairweather looked disappointed, but he nodded. "I imagine you'll find it easier to work without me banging away. Matter of fact, I ought to put things in order in my bedroom."

Put things in order meant subjecting the bedroom to the same thorough search he'd given the morning room. Still, the thumps coming from upstairs ensured that Gideon knew that Fairweather would not be interrupting him. He sat at the writing desk and, taking a moment to steel himself, set about a thorough comparison of Holford and Fairweather's accounts.

Holford's accounts were very different to Fairweather's. Neat columns tracked not only Holford's income and expenditure, but shared expenses with Fairweather and what he was owed. None of Fairweather's generosity here. Everything was added up, tallied and carried over—and it was all wrong.

Gideon stared down at the two books. The clammy feeling of his palms had migrated all over, and a distinct wave of nausea washed over him. Just as he had when uncovering Barchester Junior's deception, he had an unpleasant responsibility ahead of him. Only now he knew what he risked.

Fairweather… Only the night before he'd said that Holford was the one thing that made his circumstances bearable. To break this news was to destroy his only happiness—let alone Holford's only means of support. Could he destroy the bond the two men shared because of his pride in his word?

Gideon shut his eyes. He'd never understood how a man could keep silent in the face of injustice. Now… In ripping Holford and Fairweather apart, he would lose any claim on their friendship, a friendship that had given him the only joy he'd felt in years. And yet keeping silent and aiding a deception was impossible. It was akin to lying, making him just as culpable. Could he live knowing that he had chosen a lie?

The hair on the back of his neck prickled an instant before Holford spoke. "I don't recall giving you permission to examine my books, Lawes."

Gideon jerked to his feet, colliding with the desk. "Holford! You startled me."

Holford eyed him. His face seemed thinner and sallower than ever, his lips a tight line. "I'd like an explanation."

Gideon felt as though he'd shown up to a fencing match without a weapon. "I noticed some irregularities in Fairweather's accounts, asked if there was a way I could check them. He brought me your record book. I assumed he had your permission."

"You assumed wrong." Holford took the book from the desk and tucked it inside his jacket. "I do not tolerate my affairs being interfered with."

"I'm not surprised." Gideon swallowed, reaching for the outrage he'd felt when he'd seen the first of those neat deductions. "How long have you been cheating Fairweather?"

Holford raised his eyebrows. "Cheating?"

"You're defrauding him." Gideon waved to the record book still laid out on the desk. "Minor things here and there, a number changed in a butcher's order, an invoice for an account already paid. Taking one by one, they're negligible… But they add up."

"He owes me." Holford's voice was clipped.

"Not like this." His voice cracked—of all of it, the betrayal shocked the most. "You know how Fairweather feels about being in debt, and you're adding to it."

"He owes me this." Holford's mouth tightened. "I told you why I lost my licence. I didn't tell you who was responsible. Thank Fairweather for that. His impetuous need to see me brought him disgrace and parental approbation, but it ruined me. My training, my vocation, everything gone—and then to depend on him for mere survival." The note in his voice made Gideon's skin crawl. "He owes me much, much more than this."

Gideon took a step back, bumping into the desk. The shock of it jarred him out of his horror. "Even so. This isn't right. Yes, what happened to you wasn't fair, but taking revenge on him for it instead of addressing it… Make a clean break of it, Holford. You must tell Fairweather everything."

Holford cocked an eyebrow. "Must I?"

Gideon felt his mouth dry. His heart squeezed tight in his chest. "Either you tell him or I do."

Holford smiled, shaking his head. His eyes remained fixed on Gideon, as cold as the black ice that lay over London streets in winter. "Not happening, Lawes."

"I insist. I cannot be a party to this deception—"

Holford continued as if Gideon had not spoken. "It pains me to do this, but I cannot allow you to disrupt our arrangement. If Fairweather ever discovers the truth of our situation, it will be disastrous."

Gideon felt as if he stood on ice now. His skin was chilled to the bone and his legs shook, as if at any minute the ground might give way beneath him. "You can't stop me."

Holford said nothing. He reached into his jacket, pulling out a truncheon.

"You don't intend—" Holford was, despite everything, a gentleman! And gentlemen didn't settle their differences with violence.

Holford stepped towards him, no hesitation in his movements. Gideon turned, dashing for the door. A sharp blow caught the back of his head. He stumbled, pain crashing over him. Gideon staggered forward, dropping to his knees before the door. A little further…

No good. His vision blurred, unconsciousness fast approaching. Gideon slumped forward, crawling towards the door, trying to get as far from Holford as he could…

Scratches danced before his eyes. It took him a moment to recognise them as the marks the terrier had made in the door. But that was the study at 32 Belcairn Road. How could the dog have left marks in Holford and Fairweather's house unless—

"You lied about the house too?" Gideon rolled over, determined to face his attacker. "Just what are you playing at?"

"Pray you never find out." Holford raised the truncheon. "Goodbye, Lawes."

This time, unconsciousness was immediate.

15

"I feel responsible." The voice was familiar but, shorn of its usual ironic note, Gideon didn't recognise it. "I suggested this arrangement. I knew the risks, even if he did not… And I knew more than enough to have foreseen this."

"Dr Harris gave him a favourable report." This voice was older, mellowed with age, the distinctive blend of accents identifying the speaker at once. O'Connor sat somewhere nearby. "He's confident that not only will Lawes recover, given ample rest and peace, but that he should be himself again soon."

"He has been saying that for the last two days and Lawes remains unconscious." Westaway's reply sounded distant. Pacing? The squeak of floorboards confirmed Gideon's guess. "If Harris tells me to be patient one more time, he will need a doctor himself."

"Temper, Julian." O'Connor sounded tolerant. "You are not doing our patient any favours. Besides, he woke once."

"If you can call that waking. I—" Westaway's footsteps came to a sudden halt. "I owe the doctor an apology." This was his usual tone, the especially irritating one. "How long have you been awake, Lawes?"

Forget ghosts. Someone should investigate Westaway's uncanny instincts. "Not more than a few minutes. I wasn't sure I was awake. It feels rather like a dream." He opened his eyes.

He lay in the master bedroom of 32 Belcairn Road, curtains open to admit what sunlight London could muster. There had been changes since the last time Gideon had slept in his room. Logs were piled high on the fire with more generosity than Gideon would have allowed himself, and an armchair and side table moved in.

O'Connor occupied the armchair, and from the clutter on the side table, had been there for some time. He closed the book he was reading, and favoured Gideon with a smile. "How do you feel?"

Gideon sat up. A sharp pain pulsed from his head to his nerve endings, but after a moment, it subsided. "I've felt worse."

"You've felt better too." Westaway stood by the door, looking a touch pale, but as crisply attired as if he were stopping in on his way to a social engagement. "No, don't touch it. You got a very nasty blow to the head and you're still healing."

Gideon dropped his hand from the bandage. "Holford." The betrayal hurt worse than his head.

O'Connor looked up from the drink he was mixing. "Holford?"

"Can wait." Westaway held the door open. "You must inform the doctor his patient has awakened."

O'Connor held out the cup. "A tonic to help with the pain. Julian can help you with it—"

"I'm fine." Gideon gripped the cup. His fingers felt as if made of cotton wool rather than flesh and bone. Flexing them required concentration, but there was no way Westaway would nurse him.

Westaway closed the door behind O'Connor. He sat on

the arm of the chair the priest had just vacated. "Well, Lawes. You didn't expect your job for me to end like this."

"It's not ended." Gideon sipped the tonic. His stomach protested but, after a few careful breaths, subsided. He took a second cautious sip.

"You can't want to keep going?" The surprise in Westaway's gold eyes was real.

There was immense satisfaction in knowing he'd shattered the other's perfect poise. "I said I'd sort this out and I mean to."

"You've done all I asked." Westaway picked up a paper from the side table and waved it at Lawes. "Your reports were exemplary. Very thorough."

Gideon recognised his letter with quiet satisfaction. "I haven't found an explanation for those events. In fact, I've only uncovered further questions." His head throbbed, reminding him he was far from recovered.

"I never asked you to explain number thirty-two," Westaway said, an odd note in his voice. The irony was there, but with it a note he'd not heard before. "Just find out whether there was a ghost. From what I've read, I'd say you succeeded."

"The ghost." Gideon jerked his gaze around the room. The empty walls matched those of his waking nightmare. The tears in the wallpaper were identical. This was the room he'd lain in when he'd seen the apparition. "I've seen him."

"You have?" Westaway's stillness was that of an animal poised for action, unmoving but ready.

Gideon swallowed with difficulty, his breath sticking in his dry throat. "He was ghastly. A creeping old man standing over me as I slept."

"Can you describe him?"

Gideon nodded and regretted it—he still had a lot of healing ahead of him. "Lank brown hair, an expression of almost feverish excitement, hollow cheeks, corpse-like pallor. He wore a robe, a dressing gown, over his clothes. He had slippers too and dragged his feet as he walked."

Westaway placed a hand on his forehead. "Did your apparition use a walking stick?"

Gideon frowned. "How did you know?"

"The explanation for your ghostly sighting is at hand."

"Please, none of your riddles. My head has had all it can stand of mystery."

Westaway's expression softened. "I've asked a lot of you. At least this is one thing that we can resolve." He glanced at the door. "If I'm not mistaken, I think the solution is on his way."

"I said no more riddles—" Gideon halted. In the corridor beyond, a shuffling noise was audible, accompanied by a dull thump, like that of a stick.

He gripped the mattress, feeling the petrifying influence of the nightmare steal over him. His gaze fixed on the door. The noises drew ever closer. He watched the door handle click open, knew what waited on the other side.

The ghost stood in the doorway. He no longer carried his candle, but, just as he had the night Gideon had seen him, he scanned the room, his gaze settling on Gideon. "Allow me to congratulate you on your recovery, Mr Lawes. O'Connor has just informed me you've woken. What can we do for your comfort?"

Gideon transferred his stare to Westaway.

"Allow me to introduce my father," Westaway said, his voice even. "Despite his best attempts to the contrary, I assure you he is—" His voice hitched, a momentary wobble. "Very much among the living."

Gideon stared at the elderly gentleman. "Your father?" His head pounded, the adrenalin of moments before trapped with nowhere to go. "I don't understand."

"Mr Phillip Leighton, Lord of Foxwood." Westaway

waved a hand in the man's direction. "Inveterate ghost hunter and, in recent days, amateur nurse."

"Nurse?" Gideon repeated.

"Since Mrs Lightfoot discovered your prone body, O'Connor, Father and myself moved in, taking it in turns to sit with you. I imagine that, despite doctor's orders not to disturb your rest, father could not resist investigating your sickroom for ghosts." Westaway gave his father a pointed look.

The old man tugged at the collar of his dressing robe with affronted dignity. "I may have had a quick glance around, just to be sure that no further incidents would disturb Mr Lawes's rest."

Just like a wound throbbed when the bandage was removed, Gideon's head pulsed. "And he's not a ghost?"

Leighton drew himself up. "I may have been mistaken for a ghost before, but I am as alive as you, Mr Lawes. I don't know what my son is playing at, but you can set your mind at ease on that front."

"Oh." But he'd been so sure…

Leighton settled himself in the armchair. "That said, I am eager to hear your impressions of the house. Julian forwarded your letters on to me. I congratulate you on the detail and promptness of your communications. You'd make an excellent psychic observer. I know of many opportunities for a man of your meticulous—Julian, must you behave in that way? It is very distracting."

Westaway had turned his back to his father and Gideon. He said nothing but pressed a hand over his mouth. His shoulders shook.

Lawes blinked. Was Westaway…laughing?

Leighton eyed his son with disapproval. "If you can't control yourself, perhaps you can be useful somewhere else. I can imagine Lawes would like a cup of tea."

Westaway stood, masking his mouth with his hand. "I will

take the hint, on the condition that you don't recruit Lawes until the doctor has cleared him. Lawes, good luck."

Leighton sighed as the door closed behind Westaway. "To hear him talk, you'd think I had a one-track mind…"

"I hope you don't mind saying so, but I must confess, I am lost." Gideon wet his lips. "My head pounds, I can scarcely follow the conversation."

Leighton brightened. "I often feel that way after talking to Julian. It's impossible to have any serious conversation—but no matter. We'll say no more until you've seen the doctor. And if I'm not mistaken, I think that's him arriving now."

Gideon lay back on the pillows. He wasn't sure he'd conveyed his point, and he no longer cared to fight for it. He'd hit the limit of his bewilderment. Fairweather's revelations, Holford's betrayal, the ghost that was not a ghost and Westaway's confusing behaviour… It was all too much.

16

D r Harris was a cheerful man of advanced years, who probed Gideon's head, peered at his eyes, and ran him through the same basic questions Holford has asked on his first awakening. "Nothing to worry about," he said. "You've had a nasty bump to the head, but you're young, fit, and recovering well. Keep to your bed for the next few days, avoid agitating yourself or any prolonged mental or physical labour, and get as much rest as possible. I'll be back to check on you."

Gideon lay back on his pillows. "I'm not sure how I'll pay your fee. My circumstances at the moment—"

The doctor's brown eyes lighted on him, looking at him as a man and not a patient. There was a warmth in them that hadn't been there before. "That's already arranged, so put it out of your mind. Worry would be detrimental to your cure."

This was almost as bad as a bill he couldn't pay. "Am I indebted to Westaway or his father?"

"The responsible sort." Dr Harris shook his head as he packed up his medical bag. "While I sympathise with your desire not to be a burden to anyone, your concern is unwarranted. Mr Westaway and Lord Foxwood both insisted on paying your bill and seemed to take it as a mark of honour. Neither of them considers it a burden, so you're not to either."

"Easier said than done," Gideon muttered.

"If you feel that way about it, perhaps you should focus on recovering to deliver a comprehensive report of your experiences. Mr Leighton, in particular, wants to hear all about your experiences in the house. I'm curious myself."

Gideon mulled over the thought. "I'm not up to speaking, but I could take a stab at putting a few notes on paper."

"As long as they're only a few notes." The doctor waggled a finger at him, scolding effect ruined by the light that danced in his eyes. "Do you give me your word that you'll stop if you feel yourself becoming tired?"

Gideon smiled. Dr Harris, though a complete stranger, had such a warmth of manner that he felt he was better acquainted with the man than he was. A complete contrast to Holford! "I promise."

"Good. In that case, I'll see you're provided with paper and ink." Harris stayed to see Gideon take his medicine, and left, promising to return tomorrow.

The interview with the doctor, short as it had been, was exhausting. Gideon fell asleep. He woke to find that the candles in his room were lit, and a tray placed beside the bed with cut sheets of paper and his pen and ink-pot lying ready.

The sight of the tray warmed Gideon. Anyone in the house might have found him paper and pen, but to find his preferred pen from the desk downstairs suggested Westaway's careful attention.

Using the pillows to prop him into a seating position, Gideon inked his pen and laid his first page on the blotter. *A Brief Summary of my Experiences at 32 Belcairn Road.* He looked down at the sheet. Where to start? Moving in? Or before that, his first visit? He'd never told Westaway why he'd stumbled on the stairs. Admitting to the push now seemed like invention…

He couldn't omit anything. To do so was as good as being dishonest. Where Pettifog and Holford were involved, however, scrupulous honesty would be a gross invasion of privacy—to say nothing of the fact that Holford needed to answer for his actions. Gideon's priority should be finding Fairweather and informing him of his companion's betrayal.

Gideon bit his lip. How? He was not strong enough to leave the bed himself and asking someone else to break this news was intolerable. Perhaps he could send a message to Fairweather requesting him to visit Gideon at number 32? But no, that was also risky. Should Holford learn of Gideon's whereabouts, he might come back to finish the job. Or worse, attack Gideon's messenger. He could not risk Westaway or his other friends. There must be another way…

Gideon sighed. There was no easy solution for any of his problems.

He was still ruminating over his choices when there was a quiet knock. Westaway peered around the door. "May I come in?"

Gideon nodded, pleased for a distraction. "By all means."

Westaway poked at the fire. "I expect you're sick of being asked how you are, so instead I shall ask if you've got everything you need. Although you've probably been asked that already too."

"Not recently," Gideon said. "But I'm fine. Thank you for the writing paper." He bit his lip. How to allude to the fact that Westaway had found his pen without sounding ridiculously sentimental?

"Think nothing of it. Dr Harris mentioned you wanted to make a few notes about your experiences. Father is beside himself with anticipation. O'Connor and I banned him from your sickroom. O'Connor's taken him to the club for the evening to distract him." Westaway spoke carelessly of his father, but Gideon detected a fond note beneath the words.

"I'm afraid I didn't get far at all." Gideon hesitated. "I'm not sure how much of what happened it is appropriate to share."

"You look to have made considerable progress."

Gideon tilted his head, not sure of Westaway's meaning.

Westaway pointed to the papers in front of Gideon. "You've filled all your pages."

Gideon's gaze dropped to the tray in front of him. He gasped.

Westaway was right. The page was full of words—words he didn't remember writing. He dropped the pen.

"Easy." Westaway was beside him, placing one hand on his shoulder, one hand on the tray. "What's the matter?"

"I didn't write that. That wasn't me." Gideon stared at the page. The evidence of his handwriting and his hand clasping the pen spoke against him. "Please believe me. I have no memory of writing those words."

Westaway pushed the tray down the bed. "Where's that draught Dr Harris gave you? Swallow some."

"Do you think I'm feverish—hallucinating?" Or was he mad? To mistake pleasant if peculiar Mr Leighton for a ghost and now this!

"Whatever is going on, we will not do you any favours by getting you worked up." Westaway poured some of the draught into a cup and held it out.

Westaway's manner reassured. Gideon drank.

Westaway picked up the sheets of paper. "How does your hand feel?"

Gideon flexed it. "Sore. As if I'd just finished a solid cramming session before an exam. Why don't I remember writing?"

"Let's not get ahead of ourselves." Westaway put the pages

in order. *"A Brief Summary of my Experiences at Thirty-two Belcairn Road."*

"I wrote that." Gideon sipped the bitter draught. "I wanted to get the facts arranged in order. There are a few things I didn't tell you and I thought writing might be less taxing than talking."

"Especially when you're getting peppered with questions from my father." Westaway nodded. "That makes sense." He continued to read. *"Something is wrong. I don't know where the presentiment comes from, but the feeling comes over me that we are on the brink of some fresh disaster. It's more than a fear, a compulsion. They must not catch me unawares. I search, I know not for what."*

Gideon swallowed. "That I didn't write." His final syllable was almost a sob. It was useless to deny it. His own hand ached with having written the words. And yet…

"I believe you." Westaway didn't look up from his examination of the pages. "The writing style is not yours. Far too incoherent, and the misuse of grammar is shocking, let alone the repetition… The rest of this is all a repeat of the first paragraph."

Gideon shut his eyes. He could feel tears threatening to fall. Being believed was such a relief! But he could not let Westaway see him in this condition. "What other explanation can there be?"

"Have you heard of automatic writing?"

Gideon frowned. "What is it?"

"Not something they espouse at dear old Oxford." Westaway's mouth tightened. "A means by which a medium or person with psychic affinity has claimed to contact spirits. Because of its adoption by fraudulent mediums and hoaxers, the practice is held in disrepute, but the theory goes that the medium unconsciously provides the instrument for the spirit to write through."

Gideon stared at Westaway. He must be joking. "I'm not a medium."

Westaway cocked an eyebrow. There was no humour in his weird gold eyes. "How sure are you of that?"

17

D r Harris returned as promised the next day. "Much improved." He unhooked his stethoscope from around his neck. "I give my permission for you to spend a few hours in the downstairs sitting room provided you have someone to assist you down the stairs."

Gideon grimaced. Had Dr Harris heard about his fall? "Dr Harris, I'd like you to give me a frank answer. I prefer harsh truths to kind omissions. Speak freely."

Harris's habitual smile faded as he took in Gideon's expression. "What has Mr Leighton been saying to you?"

"It's nothing Mr Leighton said."

"He's a good sort, but he does let his enthusiasms cloud his judgement. I'm willing to prescribe no spirits or funny business if you think that will help..." Dr Harris caught himself. "Not Mr Leighton?"

"No." Gideon took a deep breath. "Tell me the truth of my condition."

Dr Harris raised his eyebrows. "We have been remiss. I assumed you knew."

"I think everyone did." Gideon gave him a slight smile. "Mr Leighton and Westaway have a habit of being casual in conversation and picking midway through. I've been so tired, I've just gone with it. But now, I must have it all clear in my head."

"Fair enough." Dr Harris drew his chair up to the bed. "Let's start with the last thing you remember before your accident."

Gideon pursed his lips. "The first accident or the second?"

Dr Harris's contracted his brow. "I was only aware of the one injury."

"Someone struck me from behind when I entered a house I mistook for this one," Gideon said. "That would be a few days ago now."

Dr Harris's frown deepened. "Go on."

"Well, the occupants of the house discovered me and took care of me. One of them had studied medicine. I was still recovering when..." Gideon swallowed. He'd only now realised what his explanation must entail. "I was struck a second time."

"That's very interesting," Dr Harris said. "Very interesting." He watched Gideon. "I understood Mrs Lightfoot found you lying unconscious in the entranceway to this house three days ago. You've been recovering since."

Gideon inclined his head. Holford could not risk Fairweather finding Gideon's prone body. He would have removed him at the earliest opportunity—and he knew Gideon's address.

"In my examinations, I only noticed the one injury."

"Would it be possible for someone, if they knew what they were doing, to strike a second blow over the first, disguising the second blow?"

Dr Harris blinked. "Possible—but very unlikely."

Gideon sank back against his pillows. Unlikely...but it was the only explanation. "Knowing I had an existing head injury, would it be necessary to give me a resounding blow to effect unconsciousness? Or would a gentler blow be sufficient?"

"How about I ask the questions?" Dr Harris interrupted. "There's something behind all these questions, isn't there? Let's have it."

Gideon looked down at his hands. "Yesterday after you left, you gave permission to have some writing paper. I had it. I sat up with it here." He looked up, searching Dr Harris's expression for some hint of awareness of what was to come. He saw none. "I wrote a sentence, nothing more. My mind was distracted by thoughts of how best to summarise my experiences. It was not until Westaway interrupted me I realised I had filled a page without being aware of it. The words were not mine."

Dr Harris whistled. It was a sound unexpected in a doctor. "When you say not yours—"

"I mean, not mine. I have no memory of writing them, they're no relation to me or my thoughts—but they were written by my hand." Gideon clamped his lips shut, fighting to control his breathing. He wanted to show Dr Harris he could handle the truth. His nerves must not give way. "There's something else. You said yourself, it was three days ago that Mrs Lightfoot discovered me unconscious here. Yet it was at least six days ago that I met O'Connor at the club. Somehow I have gained two days."

"Don't be too hard on yourself," Dr Harris protested. "You've had a great mental shock. Some confusion is expected."

"But this much? I must know. Has the blow addled my mind? Am I—" His mouth tasted of copper. "Mad?"

"If you are mad, you are the sanest madman of my acquaintance." Dr Harris grimaced. "That was in poor taste. This has been weighing on you for some time, hasn't it?"

Gideon nodded. Now that his fear was out there, the nervous excitement that had given him strength was fading fast. "Do you blame me? I am alone in the world. I must depend on my brain to earn my living. If that goes…"

"I see no reason to suspect permanent injury." Dr Harris spoke with absolute confidence. "The confusion you're experiencing is only natural. Have you any instances of losing time since you regained consciousness?"

The pressure in Gideon's chest eased. "No."

"The writing…" The doctor scratched his chin. "I admit, that's a first for me."

"Westaway said there was such a thing as automatic writing. It's a psychic phenomenon." Gideon blushed. It felt wrong even to admit that much.

Dr Harris scratched his chin, leaning back in his chair. "Did he? That seems much more his father's line."

"Mr Leighton—I mean, Lord Foxwood—agreed. He wants to have a seance." Gideon found it hard to remember the eccentric old man was a lord.

Dr Harris snorted. "Any excuse."

Gideon stared at the doctor. "You're not condoning it? You're a doctor. Science—" He stopped short.

"As a doctor, you expect me to be a sceptic?" Dr Harris said. "I look to evidence before I come to conclusions. In your case, the evidence is unclear."

"What do you mean?" Dr Harris's manner was not typical of a doctor, and yet there was something comforting in it for all that. Perhaps it was the fact that Dr Harris spoke about 'his case' as if Gideon was removed from it, granting him the means to view it dispassionately?

"On the one hand, we have your head injury. We can expect impaired judgement, confusion, headaches. Instead, you are not only coherent but give a better account of yourself than most of my patients."

Gideon forced a smile at the compliment. "That doesn't say much for your patients, Dr Harris."

He continued as if Gideon hadn't spoken. "On the other

hand, we have this house with a reputation for being haunted. You have witnessed phenomena that you have so far been unable to explain."

Gideon worried his lip. "Do you, a man of science, believe in ghosts?"

Dr Harris grimaced. "I can't say that I believe in this ghost or accept Westaway's suggestion of automatic writing. You have been exposed to the influence of this house for some time. That's bound to have an effect, even unconsciously. But I have to admit that I have come up against facts that go against all I know of reality and yet are true for all that."

Gideon stared at him. "What are you saying?"

"At this stage, I'm keeping an open mind. I suggest you do the same." Dr Harris stood, patting Gideon on the shoulder. "Do not dwell. Worrying will not solve this problem."

"Are you sure you're a doctor?" Gideon bit his lip too late. The words were out there.

Dr Harris chuckled. "I never mastered the manner appropriate to a Victorian doctor. Still, if there is room at your seance for a medical opinion, I should like to attend."

"You would? You don't think it—" Gideon hesitated. "Dangerous?"

Dr Harris cocked his head. "What makes you say that?"

Gideon picked at the blanket that lay over him. "I don't know. This house is getting on my nerves. Seeing those words in my hand was the last straw. I feel as if the worst is yet to come."

"If you feel that the seance would put too great a strain on your nerves, I shall prescribe you a complete change of scenery and total rest."

"No!" Gideon bit his tongue, ashamed of his outburst.

"No?" Dr Harris looked an enquiry.

"I couldn't leave. Not with my responsibilities unfulfilled." He had to find Fairweather and let him know what was going on. "The seance would get us closer to the truth."

"Potentially," Dr Harris allowed. "But there are other means of investigating that wouldn't require your presence."

"I should like to be there." Gideon bit his lip. "Better that than not knowing and wondering."

"That's the spirit." Dr Harris nodded, clapping Gideon on the shoulder again. "Now you get plenty of rest. If I know Leighton, this seance will be one for the books."

Gideon did not find that reassuring.

18

The terrier whined. She sat on Gideon's lap, joyous excitement at being reunited with him replaced by a determination to remain beside him. She watched with alert ears and raised hackles as Leighton bustled about, arranging the chairs around the dining room table and lighting candles.

"My thoughts exactly," Gideon muttered. He stroked her fur, watching as the rest of the participants took their seats. Leighton had tried to install him at the head of the table, but this Gideon had declined. He sat on the left-hand side of the table. Dr Harris winked at him from the opposite side. O'Connor leaned against the wall. He didn't think it was appropriate for himself to take part in the seance but wanted to be on hand 'just in case.'

Gideon had an awful feeling about that 'just in case.'

Leighton stood at the head of the table surveying his preparations. "Do you think that's enough paper, Mr Lawes?"

Gideon was trying to avoid thinking about the paper and what it implied. "Plenty."

"Where's Julian? Is he still getting ready?" Leighton frowned at the door.

"Rushing Julian in the mornings is an exercise in frustration," O'Connor observed. "He's awake, which is the fundamental thing."

"By the time he gets here, there won't be one spirit in this house, there will be five." Leighton strode to the door. His querulous tones floated back to them. "Julian, you're dressing for a seance, not a trip to the opera. What is taking so long?"

"That's the thing," Westaway's light drawl answered. "One knows what to wear to the opera. Most tailors give you a blank look when you ask about seances. I've had to improvise." He strolled into the dining room, wearing full tails complete with black gloves. A cheerful carnation tucked into his buttonhole undercut the sombre aspect of his attire.

O'Connor snorted, but his smile was fond. "A carnation with funerary blacks. Isn't that sacrilege?"

"I want to be respectful," Westaway explained as Leighton shut the door behind them and prodded his son towards the foot of the table. "We're communicating with the deceased. But I don't want to be a downer. This is why I am in such desperate need of a good valet."

"If you put as much thought into making something of yourself as you did your wardrobe…" Leighton pinched the bridge of his nose. "No, you've delayed this seance long enough. Take your place please, Julian, and not a further word about buttonholes."

As Westaway made his way down the table, the terrier stiffened. She growled, teeth bared, eyes fixed on Westaway. She barked, an explicit threat.

Gideon put his hand on her back. Instead of calming her, the gesture gave her courage to continue to bark. "I'm so sorry. I don't know what's come over her." The terrier's tiny body vibrated with suppressed excitement. "She's such an obedient dog the majority of the time."

"It's me." Westaway's smile was ironic. "Dogs don't like

me. She'll be fine once I remove myself." He sauntered to the far end of the table.

The dog rumbled. She kept a wary eye on him but lay down again on Gideon's lap.

"Are dogs usual in a seance?" Dr Harris asked. He had the air of a small boy at a party, his eyes twinkling with amusement.

"I don't see why not," Leighton said. "Animals are attuned to the psychic world, and this dog seems to be an intelligent specimen." He cleared his throat. "Before I invite the spirit present in this abode to speak, we must join hands."

"How?" Westaway asked. "I don't know if you've noticed Father, but this is an enormous table. Our arms will not reach that far."

"Come closer then. Honestly, Julian. Anyone would think you didn't want to communicate with the dead."

"Not particularly. In fact, I still think—as I told you last night—that this entire exercise is foolhardy." Julian stood, provoking a flurry of barking from the terrier.

Leighton massaged his temple. "Mr Lawes, would you mind if we put the dog outside for the duration of the seance?"

Gideon's hand tightened around the terrier. She was such an insignificant creature, it did not seem fair to leave her alone. "I'd rather not. She'll quieten in a minute."

"Perhaps you should put me outdoors," Westaway suggested.

"Don't tempt me." Leighton took a deep breath. "Let's try this again. Julian, stand next to Harris on the other side of the table and we'll join hands."

Gideon felt ridiculous. Leighton gripped one hand enthusiastically. Westaway squeezed his other hand lightly and rolled his eyes.

"Residents of Thirty-Two Belcairn Road," Leighton

began. "We have felt your presence. If you desire to speak with us, we are here and willing to listen."

They were doing this. Gideon shut his eyes, trying to concentrate.

"If you don't desire to speak with us, carry on."

"Julian, if you do not approach this with the proper amount of seriousness, I will be most displeased," Leighton said in an undertone. He cleared his throat, raising his voice. "Is there anyone here? Signal your presence with a sign."

Silence. The other men's breathing seemed loud. Gideon concentrated on keeping his own breathing even. His chest felt as if squeezed in an invisible vice, a weight pressing down on his shoulders. Was it his imagination or was the air in the room heavier?

"Spirits draw closer. We welcome you," Leighton said, his voice resonant in the small dining room. "Give us a sign that you hear us."

"Not bad," Dr Harris observed. "No one would know this was your first seance. You sound like a professional."

"No commentary," Leighton said. "Except from spirits."

At that exact moment, they heard a distinct knocking.

Gideon's eyes flew open. He saw Dr Harris draw in a breath, Westaway's frown deepen, and Leighton's expression of triumph.

"Spirits, we have heard your sign. If you desire to speak with us—"

The knocking repeated with an impatient edge.

Gideon glanced around the room. That didn't sound like a spirit.

"If I'm not mistaken," O'Connor said. "There's someone at the door. I'll let them in."

Gideon deflated, tension easing out of him. He let go of Leighton and Westaway's hands and leaned forward, putting his face in his hands.

Westaway snorted.

"Don't say a word," Leighton warned him. "I'm very unimpressed with you."

Westaway tilted his head. "You can't blame this on me?" Voices sounded in the passage outside. Westaway's expression froze. "If the purpose of the seance was to summon unwelcome spirits, then we've succeeded."

Before Gideon could ask, the terrier tensed. She focused her gaze on the door, opening to admit an apologetic looking O'Connor followed by—

"Pettifog?" Just what his morning needed.

Pettifog looked around, his gaze tightening as it took in Gideon's position, but he addressed his remarks to Leighton. "Excuse me dropping in like this. I came to give my well wishes to the invalid." His dark eyes glittered as they fell on the candles. "A seance, is it? Marvellous day for one."

Leighton brightened. "Are you familiar with seances, sir?"

"No, he is—" Westaway started.

"Tolerably familiar." Pettifog raised his voice. "Are you five? In that case, I shall be happy to make six. It is desirable for a seance if the number of participants divide by three."

"I'm only observing," O'Connor cut in.

"Even more of a reason for me to stay," Pettifog insisted. "The more energy, the greater the chance of successful communion with the beyond."

Leighton beamed. "Introduce your friend, Julian."

There was a noticeable pause before Westaway complied. "Rupert Pettifog. My father, Phillip Leighton. Dr Charlie Harris, Patrick O'Connor. Gideon Lawes—"

"I know Mr Lawes." Pettifog fixed him with a look of gloating.

Gideon mumbled a reply. Would it be unmanly to plead a headache and retreat to bed?

"We must not waste time," Leighton decided. "With Mr Pettifog making us six, let us get started."

Pettifog made a space for himself between Gideon and

Westaway. "Oh, hello, Julian," he said with a casualness that fooled no one. "This is an unexpected pleasure."

"For whom?" Westaway enquired.

Pettifog pursed his lips, but Leighton cleared his throat. "Spirits of this house, we summon thee." The seance was resumed.

19

How much of this was imagination? Gideon sat, his eyes shut. The terrier crouched on his lap, tiny body tensed for action. Did the dog pick up the tension radiating between the seance participants, or was she braced against some supernatural force?

Pettifog shifted to his right. Having gained his point and got access to the house, he was silent. His grip on Gideon's hand was tight—too tight. The room did not feel at all comfortable.

"Spirits if you are present, give us a sign," Leighton continued in a clear, calm voice.

The terrier whined.

Gideon tugged his hand free from Pettifog's grip to pat her. "All right," he whispered.

The dog didn't look at him. She stared at the table.

It convulsed.

"By Jove!" Dr Harris scrambled to his feet. "Did you feel that? The table—"

"A common occurrence at seances," Leighton assured him. "It appears we have the spirits' attention. Join hands again." He cleared his throat. "Do you wish to communicate with us?"

The room was still.

Gideon breathed out, saw his breath mist in the air. "Cold in here."

"To manifest, a spirit draws energy from the surrounding area," Leighton said, excitement barely repressed. "Look, the candles flicker. I feel sure a visitation is imminent." He let go of Gideon's hand. "Mr Lawes, take up your pen."

Gideon wiped clammy palms on his trousers and picked up the fountain pen. It felt cold and unwieldy in his hand.

Pettifog cocked an eyebrow. "I wasn't aware you were a medium, Mr Lawes?"

"Neither was I." Gideon swallowed. He would not let Pettifog rattle him.

"Let us resume the circle around Mr Lawes." Leighton directed the others to stand around Gideon, surrounding him as he sat, pen in hand. It was a clumsy arrangement, but at last Leighton seemed satisfied. "With whom do we speak?"

Gideon stared at the pen in his hand. It didn't move.

"What message do you have for us?" Leighton intoned.

As if some other hand lifted his, Gideon felt the pen move. He flinched, sending a line of ink across the page.

Leighton raised his voice. "Calm yourself, Mr Lawes. The spirits mean us no harm."

The table rattled, causing everyone to pause.

Westaway was first to recover. "You're sure of that, are you Father? Only it occurs to me that Mr Lawes has received quite some harm from the inhabitants of this house."

"Spirits only become violent when denied other means of making their wishes known. I'm sure that given the opportunity to speak, our visitant will prove no exception to the rule." He smiled at Gideon. "When you're ready."

Gideon looked at the paper, ink still bleeding wet across

it. Walking away was not an option. He owed Westaway too much for that.

Readjusted his grip on the pen, Gideon placed it on the paper. He didn't look at it. Instead, he fixed his attention on the flame of the candle nearest him.

"Whatever it is you desire to say to us, speak. We await your word." Leighton paused. "With whom do we speak?"

The pressure was back in the room, bearing down on his shoulders. Or was that the awareness that Pettifog stood behind him?

"What message do you have for us?"

Gideon gazed into the flame. With effort he could imagine himself in bed, watching the fireplace. Or perhaps he lounged on the drawing room sofa, as Fairweather bustled about, adding another coal to the gaze or satisfying himself that Gideon had all the pillows he needed—

His hand jerked, pen moving of its own accord.

Gideon averted his gaze. He would not look. He fixed in his mind the vision of the drawing room and Fairweather...

"Leave," Pettifog read out loud. "You are in danger if you remain. You put us all in danger."

"That seems straightforward," Westaway said. "Let's not keep the spirit waiting—"

"What sort of danger?" Leighton continued. "What is it you fear?"

This was a dream, Gideon told himself. In reality, he dozed on the sofa still, the crackling sound he heard not the sheets of paper as the pen scratched across them, but sausages spitting over the fire. He could not shut out the others' words, but he could insulate himself from them...

"What are you afraid of? We might help—" Leighton fell silent.

The metal nib of the pen scraped across the paper.

"Help by leaving. You can do no good here. You will wake the other."

"The other?" Dr Harris asked.

"The collector," Pettifog said. Gideon felt his gaze bore into Gideon's shoulders. "But that is a tale made up to scare children."

The pen scraped again. Gideon glanced down, saw words spilling across the paper, smudged—their communicator was too impatient to let the ink dry. "You will bring him down on us."

"Who or what is this collector?" Leighton leaned in.

Looking at the paper made him feel ill. Gideon shut his eyes.

"He is the end," Pettifog read. "The ultimate. There is no other avenue beyond him. He has no mercy, he does not tire. Leave, or I will not be responsible—and that it. He's stopped." Pettifog snorted. "I got a more helpful response from talking to the local children."

"Is that what you were doing?" Westaway's tone didn't quite match his words.

"We appear to have exhausted that spirit," O'Connor observed. "And our scribe is looking tired, don't you agree, Dr Harris?"

The doctor gave Gideon a quick once-over. "You're right, O'Connor. I think a break is in order."

"All right." If disappointed, Leighton gave no sign of it. He released Pettifog and Dr Harris's hands. "We have plenty to consider. We can resume—"

The terrier barked. She leaped to her feet on Gideon's lap, hackles on end, attention fixed on the table.

O'Connor had just opened the door. It slammed shut, the priest barely avoiding getting caught by it. The candles flared, then flickered. For a breathless moment, it seemed they'd been extinguished, but then they flickered back into life, but dim, much dimmer than they had been.

Gideon's chair scraped the floor as it slid towards the

table. As if someone had taken hold of him, his hand reached again for the paper.

"Mr Lawes, you overtire yourself," Dr Harris warned.

"I'm not choosing to do this." His voice was breathless, on the point of hysteria. Gideon felt shame, with the small part of him still detached. The rest of him was caught like his body, watching his hand move against his will. Sweat beaded cold on his arms.

The terrier jumped off his lap. She turned, barking at him. No one shushed her.

Pettifog seemed unable to move. It was Westaway who stepped forward to read the words. "You have lied," he read, and his voice didn't seem his, far too serious for frivolous Westaway. "You have claimed bonds that were not yours, you have promised and not delivered, and you have supposed too much on the kindness of others. Your account is now due. Prepare yourself."

"This is too much!" Pettifog's voice was shrill. "I'm not about to be threatened by an—an apparition! I have my pride—"

"Calm yourself." Leighton sounded eager. "There's no reason to suppose the spirit spoke to you." He cleared his throat. "To whom do you speak? A member of this party or someone else?"

"You have had ample time to repay your debts. This is your final notice. Your time is now." Dr Harris leaned forward to read the words. "Whoever this chap is, he doesn't mince words!"

Westaway took hold of Gideon's hands, prying his fingers open to make him drop the pen. "This has gone far enough. Lawes needs to rest."

The door rattled, O'Connor trying in vain to open it. "I don't think we have a choice."

The table lurched. Gideon scrambled back. Was it —rising?

"Levitation." Leighton's voice was an awed whisper. "I'd read about this, but never witnessed it—"

Dr Harris took his arm. "Let's witness this from a distance."

A splendid idea. Gideon stepped back. Westaway and Pettifog did the same.

The table didn't float. Instead, it looked more like someone hefted it preparatory to throwing it.

Gideon flung himself to the ground. He heard Pettifog's yelp, Westaway's grunt and felt their bodies collide with his. His ears rung with the crash. The air felt like a vice, squeezing the very life out of him—

"In the name of Christ, I compel thee." Nothing affable about O'Connor's voice now. It was harsh, too big for the room. "Begone, spirit, I charge thee— Leave this house!"

The entire house shuddered, an angry snarl rising from somewhere unseen. And then the pressure in the air lifted, leaving them all dazed and blinking at the dust drifting down from the ceiling.

Leighton recovered his wits first. "Julian! Are you—?"

"Fine." Was it too much to ask for Westaway to sound even slightly rattled? He stood, shaking off splinters. He removed a handkerchief from his breast pocket and dusted off his suit. "I cannot say the same for my attire."

"Confound your suit!" Leighton gripped his arm. "If you could feel the rate my heart is going!"

"Mr Lawes? Mr Pettifog?" Dr Harris approached them. "Do you need help?"

Gideon allowed Dr Harris to heave him to his feet. He looked down at the shattered wood. "It threw a table at us."

The terrier nosed his leg. He picked her up. Her small body quivered, but she'd stopped barking. She licked his neck.

"It could have killed us." Pettifog stared at the wreckage.

He transferred his gaze to Westaway, a worshipful expression coming over his face. "You saved my life."

Westaway winced. "Nonsense. Got in the way is all."

"You tackled us to the ground and took the brunt of it!" Pettifog scrambled to his feet, putting his hand on Westaway's arm. "Aren't you hurt?"

"You scarcely appear winded," Dr Harris said. "Here, let me examine you."

"No examination necessary." Now Westaway's voice held strain. "The table must have been old. Rotten. Barely bruised me."

Dr Harris pursed his lips. "I must disagree—"

"And you shall," Leighton cut in. "Later. I insist Julian takes me home at once. My health is not good, and this has been a shock. We must think of Mr Lawes, too." He turned to Gideon. "You don't object to quitting the house in the circumstances?"

Gideon was too dazed to protest.

2 0

Gideon stared at the stuccoed ceiling in confusion. The bronze light fixture gleamed like a second sun. If he turned his head, he could see curtains in an exorbitant crimson, falling all the way to the floor, and his clothes, folded across the back of a plush armchair.

Another head injury? Gideon put a hand to his forehead.

The movement disturbed the terrier, curled against his body. She lay one tiny paw on his arm to prevent him from moving and washed his hand with her tongue.

"Good dog." As Gideon stroked her ears, his memory of events returned. This was Leighton's townhouse. A guest room had been prepared for him. Dr Harris had examined Westaway, Pettifog and Lawes for injuries but, beyond cautioning that Lawes must not exert himself any further and allow plenty of time for his nerves to settle, he'd found no reason for comment.

"You are three lucky young men," he'd said as he repacked his medical bag. "To walk away from an incident like that with only bruises…"

"The table must have been rotten," Leighton said. "Old houses attract damp and rot."

Gideon pursed his lips. The table hadn't seemed rotten... But the prospect of crawling into bed and putting the events of the day behind him had been too much to resist. The words of the spirit had followed him into his dreams. *You have had ample time to repay your debts. This is your final notice. Prepare yourself—your time is now.*

Gideon winced. Ghastly. He sat with great care. His body was stiff and sore, and he could feel the beginnings of another headache. There was a bell pull beside his bed. As Gideon contemplated whether he dared ring it, there was a tap at his bedroom door.

"Now that's service," Gideon murmured to the terrier. He raised his voice. "Come in."

Leighton peered through the doorway and, seeing Gideon sitting up, bustled in. "Ah, Lawes. You're awake." He pulled open the curtains, revealing the dim grey fog of a London morning.

The terrier went rigid beside Gideon. He put a hand on her, wondering what on earth was the matter. She'd been fine with Leighton the day before, sniffing his trouser legs with great enthusiasm. What had changed?

A dog padded into the room after Leighton, a striking creature, large with silvery fur, amber eyes, and an unconcerned air. It nosed the ground, glancing up at the terrier.

No wonder she was terrified. That beast could swallow her in one gulp. Gideon put a hand on the terrier's back. "You have a dog?"

"Apparently." Leighton threw open the second of the window. "One of Julian's whims. I was about to order myself some breakfast, but I despise dining alone. Would you care to join me?"

Alone? Gideon took his gaze off the white-furred dog. "Where's Westaway?"

Leighton turned to face the bed. "Julian remembered a pressing engagement elsewhere. He gives his apologies, but states that he hopes you will stay here until you're fully recovered, a sentiment I fully endorse."

Gideon stared down at his lap. He'd thought of Westaway as a friend. The realisation he was nothing more than a convenience stung.

The white-haired dog padded over to the side of the bed, putting a paw on Gideon's side. Despite himself, Gideon stroked the dog's ears. The silvery almost-white fur made the yellow in his eyes more apparent, while there was nothing in his lean form to suggest a pampered pet. If he'd come across the beast in a forest, Gideon might have mistaken him for a wolf. As it was, he knew the dog must be one of the Alaskan breeds. A huskie perhaps? Impractical for the London climate—and so Westaway. No doubt the dog was an impulse purchase foisted on Leighton when its owner tired of it. "He's a lovely dog. What's his name?"

"What? Oh." Leighton drug a hand over his face. "Caesar."

"It suits him." Gideon studied the dog. He had a lordly air, suiting an emperor. He glanced down at the terrier. She trembled, ears pressed flat against her head. He'd never seen a more terrified dog. "Come now. It's all right. Caesar won't hurt you." He looked at Leighton. "He's well trained?"

It was a simple question, but Leighton appeared to struggle with his answer. "On the whole," he said at last. "He won't hurt your dog. In fact, Caesar." He snapped his fingers. "Make friends."

The dog looked at Leighton for a long moment and then jumped onto the bed. He put one paw on the frightened terrier's back, and, settling down beside her, started to groom the small dog.

"Breakfast?" suggested Leighton.

Gideon eased himself out of bed. The terrier's eyes followed him. "Are you sure they'll be all right?"

"Just fine," Leighton assured him. "You'll see."

Gideon ate toast in one of Westaway's dressing gowns, a liberty that he felt, even if Leighton did not.

"You're still recovering," Leighton said, pouring them both a cup of tea. "The doctor's orders were explicit. You must not overtire yourself."

Out of deference to his host, Gideon didn't protest. He ate everything put in front of him, drank two cups of tea, and made commentary on the weather. Only after a footman removed their breakfast dishes did he raise the subject on his mind. "What happens now?"

Leighton didn't need to ask of what he spoke. "Another seance, although the next, I feel, requires a medium with more experience. You're not offended, Mr Lawes? It's necessary that we restrain whatever spirits occupy the house. We must communicate with them, not allow ourselves to be threatened."

Gideon let out a slow breath. He'd not thought of it, but the seance yesterday was proof: 32 Belcairn Road was haunted. He'd fulfilled his obligation to Westaway.

Why, then, did he still feel so very much in his debt?

The thought of debt brought to mind the spirit's threat. "Aren't you afraid?"

"I will be wary, I assure you, but I believe that we have nothing to fear from ghosts. It is my earnest desire to know more about them. This…" Leighton spread his hands. "This is the opportunity I have long sought."

There was a knock at the door. A footman presented a card to Leighton. "A visitor."

"At this early hour?" Leighton raised his eyebrows. "Show them in."

Pettifog bustled in, eyes narrowing as he took in Gideon's attire. He turned to Leighton. "I had to see how everyone was after the excitement yesterday."

"How very thoughtful." Leighton motioned him to draw

up a chair. "Mr Lawes and I were just discussing our next steps."

Pettifog sat. "Julian is still recovering?"

Leighton pressed his lips together. "Julian has had to leave London, I'm afraid. An urgent matter."

Pettifog's face fell. "Will he return soon?"

Leighton winced. "He didn't indicate his plans."

Gideon stared at the two of them. He'd assumed that Westaway's abrupt disappearance was in reaction to the attack by the spirit. That had hurt, but he couldn't blame him for being scared. That table could have seriously injured them. Another possibility now occurred to him. Could Westaway have left to avoid Pettifog?

"Further investigation," Leighton was saying. "Dr Harris and O'Connor will join us here this afternoon, once the doctor has finished his rounds. We'll discuss next steps then." He turned to Gideon. "You're both more than welcome to join us."

Gideon frowned. "What do you plan to do?"

"O'Connor would like to perform an exorcism. I hope to communicate a second time with the spirit and see if we cannot help him move beyond." Leighton's eyes shone. "Actual communication with the spirit world—this isn't something we can lose."

Gideon shifted in his chair. "The risk—"

"Dr Harris will no doubt have a lot to say on that subject… But all the same, I must know more." Leighton sank into his chair, biting his thumb. A few minutes passed in silence, Leighton occupied by some pressing thought.

"And you, Mr Lawes?" Pettifog turned to Gideon.

He blinked, startled. "Me?"

"What will you do now you've confirmed the house is haunted?" Pettifog stared at him, a coldness in his brown eyes. "There is no longer any need for your presence."

Gideon's stomach churned. Pettifog had spoken out loud what he'd been trying to avoid thinking. He had no claim on Westaway or even Leighton's hospitality. There was no reason for him to stay.

21

Leighton insisted that Gideon stay with him to recover. Gideon did not protest. Westaway's absence still hurt. Revenging himself by taking Westaway up on his offer of hospitality was poor form, but Gideon assuaged his conscience with the reflection that it was upon Westaway's urging that he'd shattered his nerves. It was only fitting that Westaway's hospitality repaired him. Besides, he still had business in Belcairn Road.

Pettifog lingered, but wherever Westaway was, he'd left no clue of his location or his plans with his father. He sulked off to some unknown quarter. O'Connor called around midday and he and Leighton set off together to the library of an obscure religious institute.

Gideon declined the invitation to join them, claiming he needed to rest. He lay down only as long as it took Leighton's carriage to depart. As soon as he was confident his host had departed, he dressed, pulling on his overcoat. Turning around, he found two sets of eyes fixed on him. The terrier gazed at him, her tail a blur of anticipation. Caesar's expression was likewise hopeful, his long tail beating a slower but still optimistic tattoo.

Gideon bit his lip. He hadn't been planning on taking either dog for a walk…but it could not be pleasant for the animals cooped up inside. "All right, then. Let's go."

The townhouse was not far enough from Belcairn Road to require a cab. As Gideon tramped down the cobbled streets, he observed that the terrier had conquered her fear of Caesar. Indeed, she had increased in fearlessness, barking at dogs much larger than herself, and preening as they slunk away. That their reaction had more to do with Caesar's presence than herself did not daunt her at all.

Gideon bit his lip. She was going to be trouble.

As if thinking the same thing, Caesar glanced up at him. There was something very knowing in the dog's gaze. "Good dog." He'd never been one for animals, his uncle seeing no need for any animal that did not earn their keep. They'd had chickens and a cat to keep down the mice in the church, but a dog had been out of the question. Had Gideon been a dog person his entire life and never known it?

Gideon hunched his shoulders, turning the corner. He'd learned so much about himself these last weeks, not all of it pleasant. He was a medium, a man of peculiar needs, and most worrying of all, a man with a debt he hadn't paid. Were the spirit's words directed at him? Hadn't he imposed on Holford and Fairweather's hospitality? He'd repaid Fairweather's trust by vanishing just when the man most needed him.

"No matter." They'd reached Belcairn Road. "I'm here now." He would find Fairweather and give him the truth he deserved to hear.

The terrier ran ahead to her favourite lamppost. Caesar stayed at Gideon's side as his enquiries were met with bafflement, suspicion, or disbelief. The delivery varied but the answer was the same. No one at any of the houses had heard of Fairweather or Holford and knew of no one matching their descriptions.

Gideon staggered down the steps of the last house, his head spinning. He'd been all over Belcairn Road and received the same response. No one recognised his description of Fairweather or Holford.

How could this be possible? They must be here. Had Holford got the wind up and left? But no—that would not explain why no one knew of them.

Caesar pawed at a door and barked. Gideon clutched the nearest lamppost. His head spun. Had he imagined Fairweather? If his stint with Holford and Fairweather had been a dream brought on by his injury, or a delirium indicative of something worse…

"Stop that noise you awful d—" Mrs Lightfoot appeared in the doorway. "Here, Mr Lawes! You all right?"

Gideon pulled himself together. "Apologies, Mrs Lightfoot. I didn't see you."

"You look as bad as I feel." She motioned him inside. "Come on. A cup of tea will put you right."

Gideon sat at the kitchen table as Mrs Lightfoot bustled about. "You gentlemen have had an interesting time of things, haven't you? That dark-haired chap gave me all the news."

Gideon sipped his tea. Strong and hot and had an immediate effect. "Dark-haired… Pettifog? He's been here?"

She nodded, slurping her own tea. "Wanted to see the damage to that table." She tsked. "That ghost! The thought of what might have happened if that table had crushed one of you is enough to make my blood run cold. Which would be a disaster, on account of my rheumatism."

The table? What on earth did Pettifog want with that? Gideon lurched to his feet, making his way to the dining-room door. But where he'd last seem a mass of splinters was only a mopped and polished floor.

"None of my doing," Mrs Lightfoot said. "Not that they didn't do a good job of it. I got a shock I did, this morning, the house full of strange men, and that Mr Westaway, casual as you please, 'I hope you don't mind, Mrs Lightfoot, but finding the table rotten, I thought it best to remove it before any further damage was done.'" She sniffed. "'It's nothing to do with me, sir' I said, 'so long as Mr Hawarden knows it ain't my fault the table got broke.'" She sniffed again. "Rotten! As if I would miss a rotten table and me polishing it every week—so long as my back isn't playing up. Makes it very hard to polish, a bad back."

"Quite," Gideon repeated. He stared at the place where the table had been. It wasn't rotten… Was that why Westaway had the remnants removed? To cover up—what? The fact he was injured? Or that he wasn't?

He was going mad. First Holford and Fairweather, now this. Gideon gulped his cup of tea down. "I must go."

"Suit yourself," Mrs Lightfoot said. "As I told Mr Westaway, it makes no difference to me whether you're staying here. The ghost lets me alone."

Gideon walked down the stairs and looked at the street in front of him. The two dogs paused beside him. He knew the way to Belcairn Road. He was less certain of the way back to Leighton's townhouse.

The terrier barked shrilly.

A smartly dressed shadow emerged from an alley. "You didn't find Westaway either then?"

"Pettifog." His talent for showing up when least wanted was nothing short of phenomenal. Gideon's mouth tightened. "I wasn't expecting to find Westaway here."

"Oh?" Pettifog had perfected polite insolence. "Then what on earth possessed you to call on every house in the street?"

Caesar rumbled deep in his throat, a low sound. Gideon glanced down at him, surprised. Despite his size, the dog—save for his peculiar behaviour barking at the door before—was quiet. His growl sounded almost like a warning.

He was mad if he was crediting dogs with intelligence. "I was looking for an acquaintance."

Pettifog's smirk was sheer disbelief. "And what is this fellow's name?"

Nothing got an honest man more than being disbelieved. "Fairweather, not that it's any of your business."

"Fairweather." Pettifog looked startled. "Not the Fairweather?"

"You know him?" Gideon grabbed Pettifog's arm. "Charming, foolish, not to be trusted with an accounts book?"

"Let go. You're crushing my arm."

His hand was clamped around Pettifog's limb. He released his grip. "Well?"

Pettifog rubbed his arm. "You don't know, do you? All right. Come on." He turned, walking down the street.

"You know where he is?" Gideon jogged after him. "How?"

Pettifog smirked. "After visiting the landlord, I got a complete history of the house. I found it very interesting."

Caesar growled.

Gideon scowled. "You said it," he muttered. Pettifog was usually irritating. A Pettifog who knew something he didn't was intolerable. He wouldn't give the man any ammunition by betraying curiosity as to their destination.

Pettifog led the way in uncharacteristic silence. He walked fast enough that Gideon, not yet recovered, gained only fleeting impressions of their surroundings. He noted that the neighbourhoods they traversed were poor and growing poorer but would have been hard-pressed to identify any landmarks. The houses possessed a uniform dreariness that made identification impossible.

They reached an iron gate beyond which cracked slabs and stained headstones rested at irregular angles. Pettifog unlatched the gate and waved Gideon inside. "The St

Clement Cemetery for the Deserving Poor. Not what you'd call prime real estate."

A joke? Gideon ignored it. The terrier nosed the corner of the nearest grave. He picked her up. Somehow, her interest in the grave did not strike him as proper.

Pettifog struck out down a path which featured almost as many weeds as it did cobblestones. Gideon followed, Caesar at his heels. A shortcut to Fairweather's new house? Or had things got so bad for Holford and Fairweather that they were forced to shelter in an empty vault? He'd read of such things. If it hadn't been for Westaway's offer... Gideon's jaw tightened. He was not thinking about Westaway.

"Here." Pettifog halted.

Gideon frowned. They stood in front of a simple slab, bearing nothing but a name. No room here for one man to shelter, let alone two... His eyes fell upon the inscription, and his breath stalled in his throat.

Bedivere Fairweather
1857 – 1894

"You're not serious." Had he walked all this way to be the victim of a tasteless joke?

"I asked the landlord," Pettifog said. "And that awful old lady at the house. They both agree. There's only one Fairweather ever lived on Belcairn Road and he's buried there."

"But according to this stone, Fairweather's been dead ten years." Blood pulsed in Gideon's ears. He felt as he had the time his uncle had suggested he climb the church bell tower and check the bells for nesting birds. He'd made the mistake of looking over the edge. The same panic rose again in his chest. Gideon groped for something to steady himself, clutched the edge of the headstone. "That's impossible."

The terrier whined.

"Not impossible. Fact." Pettifog spoke with the assurance of truth.

"But I saw him, talked to the man!" Gideon protested. "This makes no sense."

"It makes sense all right. You're just too wet to see it." Pettifog spoke with deep scorn. "What kind of medium doesn't know they've met a ghost?"

22

<hr>

"There's no secret about it." Hawarden scowled at his filing cabinet. "I first read the story in the broadsheets. That's what made my predecessor buy the place. Got it cheap on account of the bad reputation. Said people would forget in time." Hawarden's scowl deepened. "More fool he. Place was going far too cheap, even for a murder."

Gideon swallowed with difficulty. "Murder?" he squeaked.

Hawarden transferred his attention from the cabinets to his guest. "Perhaps you'd like to open the window? Some fresh air—"

Gideon lurched to his feet. He leaned out the window, gulping in air that, while crisp, could not be described as 'fresh.'

Hawarden left the room. The rattle of cups and saucers followed.

Gideon tightened his grip on the windowsill. Meeting accusations of murder with cups of tea! The idea was preposterous. He remembered the prickly feeling of awareness of someone standing behind him and the sudden sharp blow to his head...

The landlord returned, tea tray in hand. "Here," he said, his voice much too cheerful. "A cup of tea will soon put you right."

Gideon leaned against the window. "What happened?"

"The usual sordid tale. Fairweather was a swell, used to the high life, made friends with a character of dubious morals. They made quick work of Fairweather's allowance and the tolerance of their mutual friends." The landlord poured two cups of very strong tea. "Belcairn Road was a last resort. Fairweather was a popular chap, so things must have been desperate."

"He mentioned being harassed by debtors." Gideon bit his tongue.

The landlord did not notice the slip. "Debts, that might be it. They were three months behind with the rent when they died. Another reason the place was so cheap. The former owner regarded the entire place as a loss." He handed Gideon a cup of tea.

Gideon had intended to refuse the cup but, having it handed to him, found its warmth soothing. His scorched palms were an antidote to the cold fog that enveloped most of him. "Holford?"

"I believe that's the name," the landlord said. "Clever chap. Not clever enough. They got him eventually."

"How?" Gideon croaked.

Hawarden stroked his nose. "Are you sure you want to hear, Mr Lawes? You appear a tad distraught."

Gideon's teacup rattled in its saucer. "I must know."

"All right. But if you'll pardon the advice, I think you'd be wise to take a rest. This entire situation appears to have a direct effect on your nerves."

Hang the fellow! What business were Gideon's nerves to him? "You said he was not clever enough?"

"Yes, well." Hawarden swallowed some of his own tea. "He was not in the house when the death took place, out carousing with friends. The friends took him home and stumbled over Fairweather's corpse, a metal strongbox lying beside it. They assumed Fairweather surprised a thief who struck him with the box. For all that he lived on the cusp of ruin, Fairweather still dressed the gentleman. Many supposed him to be of greater means than he was." Hawarden shrugged. "The matter might have rested there."

Gideon pushed past the nausea rising in his stomach. "Except?"

"Paltry things. No signs of a struggle, nor were the rooms ransacked. A friend remarked before a police officer that Fairweather's luck with accidents had run out. He'd fallen down the stairs only a month beforehand… And not for the first time, either."

Gideon sucked in a breath. Hadn't Fairweather complained of Holford's lack of sympathy when he'd suffered a head wound? "And?"

"A police officer noticed that although the furnishings in the house were 'skint,' there was a newish rug in the hall where the accident occurred. Under the rug, he found dents in the floor. The strongbox was placed above the door, so that when the unfortunate Fairweather opened it—Mr Lawes, I wish you would rest. You look positively unwell."

Gideon put his cup and saucer down on the landlord's desk. "I do not feel myself."

"Let me call you a cab." Hawarden was all concern.

Gideon did not protest. In no time at all, he was back at Leighton's town house. He fell into bed with relief.

Fairweather, not just dead. Murdered…

The mattress dipped. Caesar lay down beside Gideon, a paw resting on his back. The terrier wormed her way against his side. She licked his hand and nestled against his side.

Gideon smiled. He'd not thought of either dog since the graveyard. That they'd found their way back to the house was a minor miracle. Had Pettifog brought them? He'd parted from him in a hurry, intent on disapproving his absurd story…

Only it wasn't absurd.

Some time later, there was a knock at the door. "Mr Lawes?" Leighton peered in. "Forgive the intrusion, but I was told you were unwell."

Careful not to disturb the dogs, Gideon sat. "I do not feel my best."

Leighton peered at him. "Should I send for Dr Harris?"

Gideon shook his head and regretted it. His head still ached when moved suddenly. "I may have taken too much exercise than was good for me."

Caesar, sitting up on the bed, barked.

Leighton gave the dog a sharp look. "Get off the furniture." He waited until Caesar, taking his time, complied, and then looked straight at Gideon. "Is that all, Mr Lawes?"

Gideon hesitated. His honest nature would not allow him to lie in response to so plain a question. Besides which, Mr Leighton might be the one person who could help in this situation. "I received something of a shock. I told you I suffered two head wounds?"

"Yes, though I admit I don't quite see how it was possible in the time between your collapse and O'Connor finding you," Leighton replied.

Gideon waved him towards a seat. "While I was unconscious, I suppose I dreamed…" It had to be a dream, didn't it? "That I was the houseguest of two men named Fairweather and Holford."

Leighton caught his breath. "You don't say." His eyes gleamed, and he pulled his armchair over to Gideon's bedside. "You saw them?"

"And spoke to them." Gideon studied his benefactor. Leighton's interest was unrestrained. It didn't seem decent somehow. "I cannot prove it was not mere delusion, but there are instances—things said—that tally with the facts as given me by the landlord."

"So you've spoken to Hawarden?" Leighton didn't sound annoyed. "Is it there you received your shock?"

"Yes. You see…" Gideon realised his hands were knotted in the bedsheets. He released the fabric, smoothing it back into place. "I did not until then believe they were dead."

"Interesting," Leighton said. "Very interesting." His gaze rested on Gideon. "And now?"

"I can still scarce believe it." Fairweather was so lively, it was impossible to think of him as dust and bones these last ten years. And Holford… Gideon's blood ran cold. Holford had asked for his address and date and not commented. Did Holford know?

To be dead and not know it was one thing. To be dead and know… Gideon shuddered.

"I'm not so sure you shouldn't have Dr Harris. This shock has hit you hard." Leighton stood, Caesar standing with him.

Gideon grabbed his arm. "Don't go." He looked down at the bedcovers, ashamed of his action. Even the terrier looked at him in surprise. "I must know. You're an expert in the paranormal. Is it possible that—while I was unconscious—I saw them?"

Leighton sank back into his armchair. "It's impossible to say for sure, Mr Lawes. Knowing you are an honest man, and, until recent times, a sceptic, I believe you experienced something of the spiritual world."

The terrier nosed Gideon's hand. He patted her. "Something?"

"The study of the supernatural is yet in its infancy. I should not like to make any surmise beyond that."

"So you can't—" Gideon bit his tongue too late.

"Can't?" Leighton prompted.

Gideon swallowed. "Can't tell me how to see them again."

Caesar's low growl broke the silence that followed this statement.

"No," Leighton said. "I can't. To do so would be most foolhardy, given the consequences of your previous interactions with the occupants of number thirty-two. You must give the idea up."

Gideon sank back against his pillows. Leighton had been his only hope. If he said it was impossible...

Leighton heaved himself onto his feet, leaning on his walking stick. He patted Gideon's shoulder. "What you want is a complete distraction. I'll bring you some light reading. But first, I must get these dogs fed. Come, Caesar." The dog was already on his feet. "Come... " Leighton looked to the terrier.

"Cleo," said Gideon. "Short for Cleopatra." He nodded to Caesar. "It seemed fitting." In Caesar's company, the little terrier behaved as though she were a queen.

Leighton smirked. "Come, Cleo."

The terrier followed. Apparently she knew that food was in the offing. Or was it Caesar's presence? The bigger dog tolerated her and, previous fear forgotten, the terrier considered him as much a friend as Gideon himself.

Gideon was still musing on the mutable affections of small dogs when a knock at the door heralded Leighton's return.

"The light reading I promised you," he said, putting a pile of books on Gideon's bedside table. "I'll endeavour to keep you free from visitors this afternoon."

"That's all right," Gideon started, but Leighton shook his head, held a finger to his lips, and hobbled out the door.

A most unaccountable man. Gideon was no longer surprised that Westaway was as hard to decipher as he was. With Leighton as his father, the odds were against him from the start. He picked up the books and got another surprise.

The first two books in the pile were fashionable novels of

the moment, but the third came from Leighton's own collection. *On Communication with the Spirit World...* Gideon traced
a hand over the cover. Was Leighton encouraging him? But
he'd recommended against trying to contact Fairweather.
Gideon glanced at the door. Was Leighton's assurance that
Gideon would be undisturbed encouragement to revisit the
house?

Only one way to find out. Gideon opened the book.

G ideon unlocked the front door, listening for the tell-tale sound of a mop or creaking joints. Mrs Lightfoot had completed her daily tasks and had departed. The house was as quiet as—as, well, a tomb.

Gideon winced, shutting the door behind him. The sounds or lack thereof had not troubled him before he'd known of number 32's past. Was he now the victim of an overactive imagination? He must approach this in the proper mental state. *Communication with the Spirit World* was clear. To obtain the desired response from the spirit world, one must communicate with an open mind and a lot of candles. These last Gideon retrieved from the pantry.

He entered the dining room only long enough to retrieve the candleholder. After his previous experiences, he would not remain in there a second longer than he needed to. No, the morning room was his object.

The sofa and chairs were not as he last remembered them. Someone had gathered his papers together, and a few French novels and a book of sermons on the bookshelf showed that O'Connor and Westaway had used the room during Gideon's convalescence.

No matter now. Gideon turned to a fresh page of paper. His hand shook as he lit the candles, but his voice was steady. "Spirits of this house, I summon thee." What had Leighton said next? "I urge you to speak. I'm listening."

No sound followed this announcement, not even the usual creaking of aged timbers. Gideon relaxed the hand that gripped the pen. According to *Communication with the Spirit World,* a seance was most successful when there were three or more people gathered. Gideon was alone. What if whatever medium qualities he possessed were insufficient for the task?

He had to speak to Fairweather. Gideon concentrated his attention on picturing the man. Fairweather seated at the desk, his sunny expression clouded, lips pursed as he wrestled with his accounts. Turning to share a remark with Gideon. Laughing at his own foibles. That such a man could be dead wasn't right—

The pen jerked in Gideon's hands. He kept his eyes fastened on the mantelpiece, not looking down at his hand. Only when the spasm had passed did he dare look at the paper.

He saw a column of sums, numbers crossed out and tallied as Fairweather did his adding up.

Still trying to balance his accounts. Numbers gave Gideon a feeling of security, but staring at these sums, he felt nothing but helpless. The final balance was lacking. Was that what kept Fairweather in the house?

The pen scraped against the paper again. Fairweather had resumed his account keeping.

"Fairweather," Gideon said. "Do you hear me? Please. You need to stop."

The pen went on, unheeding.

"It's me, Lawes. I must tell you something."

The column of numbers continued.

Gideon took a deep breath. He placed his left hand over

his writing hand, preventing it from moving. With both hands, he directed the pen across the paper. *Fairweather, stop,* he wrote. *It's me, Lawes.*

The resistance in his right hand stopped. The flames of the candle flickered.

Had he got Fairweather's attention? Gideon took a deep breath and wrote his next sentence, speaking it out loud as he did. "I need to talk to you."

His breath misted in the morning room. A good sign. *Communication with the Spirit World* shared Leighton's view that spectral beings required energy. If this was Fairweather's presence—

The pen flew out of his hand, flying across the room and splattering ink against the wall. Gideon hastened to his feet with a cry of dismay. The stain—

A tearing sound drew his attention to his hands. He ripped the paper in front of him in half, bundled the halves together, and ripped them again. He repeated this action until he reduced the paper to fragments. Only then did the controlling force leave.

Gideon let the last scraps of paper fall and staggered over to the window. He fought with the sash, heaving it up, and leaning outside. His hands gripped the windowsill.

His knees shock. The spirit's passing left his body weak. Had the automatic writing drained his energy as well as the candle's? Gideon turned his head to see how they fared.

The candles had been fresh when he lit them but had melted down to half their length. Their flames leaped higher, making quick work of the remaining wick. Again, Gideon felt the temperature cool as pressure built within the room.

A hand locked around his throat, tilting his chin up. As Gideon gasped for breath, his hands rising to wrestle it free, the grip tightened.

"Do you have any idea what you're doing?" Holford's

voice was low, but the anger in it immediately audible. "You will destroy him."

Gideon shut his eyes. What terrified him more: the thought Holford might stand beside him, or that he might not? "Fine words from his murderer!" The thick tang of tobacco that accompanied Holford was genuine enough. "You killed him!"

Holford's fingers tightened almost to choking point. A second later, he relaxed his grip. "And have had ample time to regret it. You do not know the danger you pose."

"Danger?" Gideon's voice hitched. He made another attempt to tug himself away from Holford's grip. "You're strangling me!"

"You ridiculous pup. Have it your way." Holford shoved him towards the window. His footsteps echoed across the floor, but of Holford himself there was no sign. "Will you listen now?"

He was somewhere near the desk. Gideon felt sick. He rubbed his neck, still throbbing where Holford's fingers had been. "It's not you I want to speak to. Fairweather must know the truth."

"The truth will destroy him." The candles flickered. There was little tallow left. They would be burnt up entirely in minutes. "Listen, Lawes. You're a good man. Better by half than me. But what you intend… Don't you see that he doesn't know?"

Gideon swallowed. His ghastly surmise was true then. Holford was aware of his fate. "You do. You're able to accept it. Fairweather—"

"I don't have Bedivere's belief in his honour or his horror of unpaid debts." The air grew thick with tobacco. Had Holford lit a pipe indoors? He must be rattled. "For me, death is unpalatable but a truth I accept. For Bedivere, it is a failure so stark that he has blinded himself from it all these years."

Gideon looked down at the scraps of paper, shuffling on

the ground, disturbed by some unseen movement. "Not entirely. His behaviour, constantly looking over his accounts…" *Communication with the Spirit World* indicated that ghosts obsessively replicated their behaviour in life. "You must see the anguish that causes him. Truth—no matter how unpalatable—must be better than an eternity striving after an impossibility." Gideon swallowed. "You loved him, once. You cannot in all conscience leave him to this fate."

The air grew chillier. Gideon glanced behind him to the half-open window. If all else failed, he could hurl himself into the street.

Holford's sigh made the candle flames flutter. "It is because I loved him, once, that I would spare him an even worse fate. Your belief in the truth notwithstanding, there is another you must take into account—the third occupant of this house."

Gideon's brow furrowed. "A third?" Did Holford include Gideon in his calculations…

"The Collector." The sneer in Holford's voice didn't quite ring true, undercut by a wobble. Fear? "He comes for those who have left debts behind them."

Gideon's hands tightened into fists. "Is it Fairweather you're concerned for or yourself? What are a few unpaid bills compared to murder?"

"It doesn't work that way. Debt is in the beholder's eye." Papers shuffled as Holford shifted, his voice growing dim. One candle spluttered and died. "I paid for my crime. A life for a life—and more. I knew my fate. Waiting in my cell for that final walk, I died dozens of times. No, it's not me he's after."

A chill prickled across Gideon's skin. "Fairweather?"

"Bedivere believes he still has time to make good his debt. Were he to know the truth, his despair would call the Collector upon him in an instant. He would be devoured, utterly destroyed." Holford's voice was all but a whisper.

"And if I, the person who has more reason to resent him than any other, do not wish that fate for him, still less reason one who loves him should destroy him."

Gideon jerked backwards. "Loves him?"

The room was quiet. The last candle burnt out with a hiss. Gideon released a shuddering breath. Loves him… It was true, dash it all. And with this truth was one other: Gideon must leave Fairweather to his fate or destroy him.

24

Gideon's departure was noticed. When he joined Leighton and O'Connor for dinner, his host greeted him with a gleam in his brown eyes. "You found your reading matter instructional then?"

Gideon pressed his lips together in what he hoped would pass as a smile. "It was most educational."

Leighton's expression brightened. If Gideon had not seen him leaning on his cane, he would have thought him a much younger man. "What news do you have?"

O'Connor looked up. "I understood Mr Lawes was resting."

"You can't expect someone to rest with a mystery like this still unsolved." Leighton tugged Gideon's chair out from the table. "Tell us all."

O'Connor winced. "And you're surprised Julian is so wilful?"

Leighton ignored this remark. "Well?"

Gideon sat. He did not feel like sharing his discovery. On the other hand, he was indebted to Leighton—and there was every chance Leighton would not rest until he sated his curiosity. "I've spilled some ink in the morning room."

"Julian can deal to it," Leighton said. "Writing?"

"Yes."

"Holford again?"

Had it been obvious to everyone at the seance but him? "No. Fairweather—at least to start." Gideon worried his lip. "I think I startled him. Holford took over."

"At your direction or his?" Leighton asked.

Gideon blinked. It was not the question he'd been expecting. "His."

"You were trying for Fairweather then? I wonder..." Leighton studied him with an expression Gideon didn't know how to read.

The footman entered with the first course. A necessary pause occurred. Gideon was about to protest as his glass was filled, but hesitated. After his experiences that afternoon, he needed, as Mrs Lightfoot would say, a stiffener.

"Did you learn anything new from the conversation?" O'Connor asked once the footman left.

Gideon toyed with his glass. "Only that Holford fears the Collector." A ghost afraid of a ghost. There should be something humorous in that, not this interminable feeling of failure. He gulped his wine, nerving himself against the next question.

It didn't come. Instead, O'Connor turned to Leighton. "I've had word from Wiremu."

Leighton looked disappointed but was too well-bred not to take the hint. "Good old Bill. Well? Is he joining the fun?"

"He says that we can count him out. Ghosts as you know—"

"He doesn't mean to avoid all ghosts?" Leighton protested.

O'Connor sliced his veal into neat, even pieces. "He is firm on the subject. Wiremu has very definite ideas of the respect appropriate for the dead."

"And very definite ideas of the proper way for a

gentleman of leisure to pass his time! We won't see him until after the racing." Leighton shook his head and turned to Gideon. "What's your vice, Mr Lawes?"

"I beg your pardon?"

"Do you follow the horses? Hunt? Or perhaps you are a sporting lad." Leighton considered him. "You look an active chap."

Him, an athlete! "I walk. I have got rather in the habit of it." His carriage had been the first thing to go after the disaster, followed by his groom. Now, even an omnibus was an unaffordable luxury.

"If you ever fancy a spot of hiking, you must let me know," Leighton said. "There are some rather good trails around Foxwood, and Julian has never, to my knowledge, refused a ramble. You must visit us sometime."

And be even more in Leighton's debt? Gideon mumbled something about kindness.

"Nonsense." Leighton beamed at him with the air of a country lord conferring a boon. "It would be a pleasure. You London dwellers don't realise what a challenge it is to fill the days in the countryside. A visitor is always welcome, especially one that gets along with Julian so well. If he were here now, he would agree."

Gideon almost choked on his veal. Westaway thought so little of him he'd abandoned him without a word of farewell! Was this a joke on Leighton's part?

But no, Leighton extolled the virtues of the English countryside and Foxwood's park and gardens with no trace of irony. Strange.

O'Connor seemed to sense his confusion. The conversation turned to literature and, when Gideon admitted that he'd not had much leisure for reading recently, to theories of education. Had O'Connor glimpsed Gideon's tentative essay? He did not allude to it, talking instead of the various qualities looked for in a teacher. Leighton joined in with reminiscences from his school days, and Gideon ventured a memory or two of Westaway at Oxford. The meal was pleasant enough and the food superb, but Gideon saw the dessert tray carried away with a sense of relief. He had much to think about—provided his whirling thoughts would give him any relief.

Caesar and Cleo were curled up on his bed. Caesar had dragged the blankets into a nest and dozed, Cleo sitting beside him, grooming one giant paw. Both dogs looked up as he entered, the terrier dancing up to him. Gideon sat, ruffling her ears. It was a sad day when the dog's obvious delight to see him did not touch him in the slightest.

Fairweather had been so happy. And Fairweather was worse than dead, trapped in an existence without joy and with no possibility of release. "Fairweather..."

Caesar whined.

The knowledge in the dog's amber eyes struck Gideon as uncanny. "It's almost as if you understood."

A brisk knock at the door. "Mr Lawes? A word if you don't mind." O'Connor's lilting tone made the intrusion less abrupt.

"Come in." Gideon waved him towards the armchair.

O'Connor remained standing. "You're a sensible chap, Mr Lawes, which is why I hope you won't take what I'm about to say amiss. Leighton is a dear friend,but he can be very... short-sighted in pursuit of a goal, and a trifle inclined to impose. You must be firm with him. He takes no offence, I can assure you. If you find yourself reluctant, send him to me. I am more than happy to refuse on your behalf."

"A kind offer, Mr O'Connor, but I don't need to take you up on it. I won't be returning to the house."

The terrier nudged his hand with her head. He stroked her ears. What Holford had told him was too awful to contemplate. Much too awful to speak out loud.

O'Connor sat in the armchair Leighton had occupied that morning. "What happened at the house this afternoon?"

Caesar sat up, shaking off his sleep. He nosed Gideon's free hand.

Gideon stroked his ears. "I don't know if I should tell you. I feel there is nothing I can do… And yet…"

"Tell me," O'Connor said. "You may find comfort in being listened to."

"All right." Gideon plunged into his story.

O'Connor sat as Gideon spoke, scarcely even moving. As he listened, the furrow in his forehead increased.

Gideon's heart sank. It was just as he feared—hopeless. "So there is nothing that can be done without inflicting upon Fairweather an even worse fate."

"I wonder," O'Connor mused.

Gideon looked up. "You're not suggested we loose this Collector on him?"

"Nothing so extreme," O'Connor said. "I merely suggest that the situation is not so black and white as it seems. Holford was young when he died?"

Gideon blinked. "About the same age as myself, I should imagine."

"Young men, in my experience, have very fixed views of right and wrong. It is all or nothing for them. Holford believes the situation is hopeless, therefore it is."

"But Fairweather… I don't think you realise just how deep his fear of dying in debt goes." Gideon sagged forward. "He would never forgive himself—any more than I will forgive myself for acquiescing to this lie."

O'Connor laid a hand on his shoulder. "Take heart, Mr Lawes. As someone who was once young and miserable, I can say that sometimes it is better to be kind than to be just. Forgive yourself. Fairweather, were he aware of the situation, would not blame you."

Gideon winced. Fairweather wasn't aware of the situation. He must believe that Gideon had abandoned him, just as Westaway had abandoned him.

"Rest," O'Connor continued. "I will tackle Leighton once more about an exorcism. It is time that all the occupants of thirty-two Belcairn Road moved on." He nodded and made his way to the door. Caesar jumped off the bed, following him.

Gideon lay back on the bed. The terrier settled beside him, washing his hand with her tongue.

Time the occupants of 32 Belcairn road moved on. Was exorcism any better than leaving them to the Collector? If he could only talk to Fairweather, one more time... "Like that would do any good." He couldn't explain his absence without telling him the truth. Gideon was incapable of lying...

Incapable? Gideon sucked in a deep breath. He'd never lied in his life, not knowingly. His honesty was as much a part of him as the colour of his hair or eyes. To lie went against everything he stood for.

Unbidden, the memory of Fairweather on his knees searching for loose change came to mind. Honesty couldn't help Fairweather. A lie might be his only chance.

To slip out of the townhouse, Gideon had to pass Leighton's room. He scuttled past but wasn't able to avoid hearing a snatch of conversation.

"—what a chance this is." Leighton's voice was raised. "Confirmed presences—and they communicate! What we learn—"

"Will not help Thomas." O'Connor was firm. "And will not help those poor souls either. We have the means to end their suffering. Why delay?"

A bark punctuated his sentence, Caesar adding his tuppence to the conversation. Gideon shook himself and hurried onwards. For all his apparent intelligence, Caesar was just a dog. More likely seeing his owner in argument upset him.

Gideon walked out the townhouse door before the footman could enquire if he needed a cab. He could not lose his nerve. If O'Connor convinced Leighton that an exorcism was the right thing to do—well, he didn't have time to think twice.

As he turned down Belcairn Road, Gideon met a cart

going the other way, the night soil men on their usual round. It was later than he'd realised.

He unlocked the door to 32 Belcairn Road. "Fairweather! Holford!"

His voice echoed through the empty house. Gideon opened the door to the morning room. Empty. He hurried up the stairs. "It's me, Lawes. I need to speak to you." The bedroom was likewise deserted. There was no trace of anyone in the house, not even a scurrying rat.

He'd not thought to bring candles with him. Gideon made his way downstairs, hand clamped to the bannister out of habit. Had those been Holford's hands he'd felt in his back? Was he doomed to repeat his actions, just as Fairweather was doomed to his fruitless accounts?

Gideon caught his breath. Holford had attacked him that night, his blow plunging him into the ghost's world. His eyes fell on the wooden floorboards of the reception, still bearing the dents of the trap that had claimed Fairweather's life. It had worked once…

The frying pan missed Gideon, bouncing off the floorboards. Gideon balanced it above the door. Too light? He needed something that would knock him out, but not do serious damage. He had no intention of being the third death in the house…

Ice gathered between his shoulder blades, a chilly breeze travelling down his neck. "I'd not pegged you as a suicide," Holford remarked. "Or is this a social call?"

Gideon yelped. His elbow collided with the door, sending the frying pan crashing to the floor.

Holford looked down at it. He was visible in the parts of the hallway lighted by the streetlamps outside. The emptiness of the shadows suggested that he was not entirely there.

Don't think too hard about it. Gideon inhaled, feeling the cold night air deep in his throat. "I need to see Fairweather."

"Impossible," Holford said. "The truth will destroy him."

"I'm not here to tell him the truth." His cheeks heated, his admission sour on his lips.

Holford studied him. "What good do you think this will do? You can't change anything."

Gideon shut his eyes. The last person on earth he wanted to be in debt to was Holford, but he didn't see any alternative. "I might. Holford, I think I know a way to free Fairweather. But I must see him. Will you help me?"

Holford stepped closer. It took all Gideon's willpower not to shrink away from him. "What you suggest is impossible. Don't you think I've been over it in my mind thousands of times?"

"Let me try," Gideon rasped. The hallway resembled a frosty winter morning. Every breath scraped his throat with cold. "If it doesn't work, you'll be no worse off than you were before."

Holford glanced upstairs. His smile was sardonic. "Against my better judgement, I will give you my aid. I hope you know what you're doing—for all our sakes." He stepped closer to Gideon until another step would end in collision.

"What are you—" Holford didn't slow. Cold shot down Gideon's body as Holford stepped into him. His vision swum with white light, his head throbbing with pain from his injury. He swayed, grasping for the stair bannister. His hand grasped empty air, and he stumbled backwards, landing on the stairs.

"Holly? What are you—" Fairweather appeared at the top of the stairs holding a candleholder. He wore a nightshirt, a dressing gown wrapped around him. His face lit up. "Lawes! What a pleasant surprise—but your health? Holford told me he advised you to put yourself in the care of an expert."

Fairweather didn't resent his absence? Gideon exhaled. "I had to see you."

"So I gathered." Fairweather pursed his lips, one hand reaching for the staircase bannister. "Are you psychically inclined? A very rum thing happened this afternoon."

Gideon heaved himself to his feet. The ache in his head pulsed. A reminder that this was only temporary? Despite the pain, warmth rose in his chest. "Why don't you tell me about it in the morning room?"

Fairweather bustled about, making a cup of tea and fetching pillows to make Gideon more comfortable. Gideon could not deny him, knowing this would be the last time they spent together. He looked around the morning room, just as he'd last seen it in Fairweather's company. Did the ghosts control the house's appearance?

"Holly would choose now to go for a walk. How provoking of him! Never around when you want him." Fairweather chattered away. "He'll be astonished to see you. He was very insistent that I not expect to hear from you again, and here you are."

"Here I am." Gideon gripped his cup of tea. It was all he could do to keep his hands from shaking.

"Everything is all right, isn't it?" Fairweather sat at his desk, his own cup of tea beside him. "It was such a strange thing this afternoon... And now you show up! It's, well." He laughed, but the sound was a poor imitation of his customary amusement. "A bit too coincidental."

Fairweather was nervous too? Gideon's heart leaped. He put his cup of tea aside. He could delay no longer. "I had a realisation this afternoon. About you. Well, actually, it was about your finances."

Fairweather blinked. With his eyes open wide, and his blond curls sleep tousled, he looked more like an overgrown boy than ever. "My finances?"

"You remember that your accounts puzzled me." Gideon nodded to the book lying on Fairweather's desk. "This afternoon, it occurred to me that there was a very simple solution to the discrepancy I had noticed." He held out his hand. "May I?"

Fairweather handed him the accounts book. "This afternoon, I was sitting here doing my accounts when I had the strangest feeling that you were here in this room. I turned around to make a remark, forgetting that you'd left us. It was a shock to see your sofa empty, and an even greater shock to turn back to my accounts and see a message in your handwriting. Holford said it was a subconscious desire to see you, but I wonder…"

The sofa was Gideon's sofa now, was it? Conscious that his face was heated, Gideon jotted down his notes in the book as quickly as possible. "I've never thought of myself as psychic. My uncle was very much against such things."

"We've had a very peculiar time of things since you left us," Fairweather continued. "The ghost has been active enough for three men, and the dining room table repossessed. Rather rude, I thought, not to give us any notice, but it gave us a respite. Holly could even do some shopping. We've been dining like kings and drinking madeira every night."

Nice to know that Westaway's generous stocking of the pantry was not wasted. "I'm glad." Gideon raised his head, meeting Fairweather's eyes. "I've been thinking a lot about you."

Fairweather's smile was impish. "And my accounts."

Gideon ducked his head in acknowledgement. "It's just as I thought. In your desire to make sure you were on top of your debts, you have doubled up on some charges. Here is your actual balance." He held out the accounts book.

Fairweather looked down at the new total, and his expression changed. "But this puts me in the black! You don't—you're not mistaken?"

Gideon's chest felt like a vice squeezed him. "I'm not

accustomed to making mistakes of this nature." He'd never lied, not once. He was astonished at how natural he sounded. "Your arithmetic, on the other hand..."

"Say no more." Fairweather's mouth smiled, but he had to blink. "I—Lawes, you don't know how much this means."

Gideon's eyes prickled. He looked away. "I think I have some idea."

"I needn't be afraid to step outside the house now. A marvellous thing. I was having some very peculiar ideas." His laugh was a little too breathless, and the hand that squeezed Gideon's shook. "I don't know how to thank you."

"You don't need to." Gideon put his arms on Fairweather's shoulders. "After all the care you took of me, this is the least I could do. Don't give it a second thought—I beg you." If Fairweather looked too closely at his accounts, everything would be for naught.

"It's not everyone who would go to this much effort over my accounts." Fairweather wrapped his hands around his accounts book. "You—care a lot about me."

Gideon's brain stalled. "I—"

"I'll remember this always, Lawes." Fairweather leaned in, lips pressing against Gideon's cheek. The touch was as light as a whisper, and then there was nothing more, just a lingering warmth and the thud of the accounts book hitting the floor.

Fairweather was gone.

Gideon sank back onto the sofa. He reached for the accounts book, replacing it on the desk. He took a last look around the morning room, fire still burning in the grate, steam rising from their untouched cups of tea. He lingered in the room. Bare of all but the most basic of comforts and yet, he had been happier within these walls than he'd ever been before...

The curtains lashed against the window, whipped by an icy breeze. The flames jumped before they died, illuminating the figure standing before the door. Even in the darkness, that image remained before him. Black suit in rags, blanched white finger bones tightened around the noose he held. A skull regarded him, hollow eyes reflecting the implacable approach of death. The Collector had arrived.

26

"You're too late." Gideon's breath misted as the temperature in the morning room plummeted. "Fairweather's beyond your reach."

The room was pitch black except where squares of light from the streetlights outside fell through the windowpanes. Gideon didn't need to see the Collector to know where he was, or that he'd stepped towards him.

Gideon retreated. "You'll never take him."

I collect a debt owed. The words weren't spoken, but Gideon heard them all the same. They trickled through his brain like ice. *Your time is up, Gideon Lawes.*

"My time?" Gideon bumped against the wall. "I owe you nothing."

Movement in the shadow to his right. Gideon's skin crawled with the unnatural chill. *Fairweather's debt is yet unpaid. I claim your life in payment.*

Gideon darted to the left. If he could just make the door—

The noose tangled around his legs. He crashed to the ground. Gideon kicked himself loose, only to feel a bony grip on his neck.

"This isn't right—you know this isn't right!" Gideon

clamped both hands around the skeletal hand. "You can't just decide what's right and wrong!"

I collect what is owed. There was nothing in that voice, not even satisfaction. The Collector stated his truth as if it were inevitable.

Perhaps it was. The cold of the Collector's touch travelled beneath Gideon's skin, penetrating his veins. His hands responded sluggishly to his thoughts, his grip loosening.

Your honesty does not protect you now. You lied, Gideon Lawes.

"To save a life!" The cold reached his heart. Gideon shut his eyes, gasping as pain seared his chest. An icicle stabbed through the heart could not hurt more—or chill more—than this. "Does that mean nothing?"

A life for a life. The skeletal grip tightened. *I will take what I'm owed.*

"It won't work." Gideon sagged forward. His consciousness was fading fast. Every breath tore at his throat like a razorblade, the cold air stinging his lungs. His body throbbed as if in the early stages of frost bite. Gideon knew with perfect certainty that he was dying. "A balanced account book can't reflect things like life or love, a smile, compassion… all the things that make life worthwhile." Honesty alone wasn't enough. A tear ran down his cheek at the thought of all the opportunities he'd never seen, wedded to his superior morality. "It's people…"

Gideon slumped forward, no longer resisting. If this paid Fairweather's debt, so be it. At least he'd done something worthwhile with his life. "Fairweather…"

Warmth surrounded him. The pain faded, replaced by a gentle pressure. Gideon felt himself cradled in a warm embrace. A last illusion before death claimed him? There were far worse ways to go…

A debt is a debt. The Collector's calm had faded. *Yours must be paid, Bedivere.*

"Your balance sheet is one-sided."

Gideon's eyes flew open in shock. That was Fairweather's voice!

Fairweather knelt on the morning room floor, arms clasped around Gideon. Gravity gave his face an unusual nobility. He stared at the Collector, voice firm. "Where are hours of labour, of care given to friends without a thought of repayment, of friendship, of love, of companionship? All the things that make a life more than a life."

What of carelessness and errors of judgement? The Collector's fury rattled the house. *What of that? No, only one thing can make atonement. Your life—or his.*

Gideon shivered. "It's no good. Reasoning won't work." Ghosts were inflexible, unable to change. Until he had his due, nothing would satisfy the Collector.

Fairweather's mouth twisted. "I did not think this through."

Gideon shut his eyes. The admission was so Fairweather it hurt. He pulled himself into an upright position. "What made you come back?"

Fairweather helped haul him to his feet. "You. A Fairweather does not leave a debt unpaid. This…" He squeezed Gideon's hand.

"No debt," Gideon croaked. The cold encroached fast. Even when he put both arms around Fairweather, he couldn't block out the chill. "You gave me so much. I did not know what life was before I knew you."

The bitter wind enveloping them battered Fairweather's blond curls and whipped his cheeks red. He blinked, one hand cupping Gideon's cheek, ignoring the storm overtaking them. "Lawes—"

"Gideon." His vision blurred, white spots dancing across his eyes. He kept them open, fixed on Fairweather's face. If he could choose nothing else, at least he could make his last sight worthwhile.

"Gideon," Fairweather said. "I cannot think of anyone I'd rather breathe my last with."

Fairweather had not drawn breath for more than a decade, but Gideon did not point that out. His thoughts were slow. It could not be much longer now. He regretted nothing. If he could not live with Fairweather, then dying with him was all that he could hope for.

"In the name of Christ, I compel thee." A strident voice cut through the frosty air. "Begone spectre. You have no power here, and no claim over the living."

The Collector shrieked. The house shook, the floorboards rocking beneath Gideon's feet. *You dare! You're not even a real priest!*

"Real enough," O'Connor said. He stood in the doorway, holding a bible against his chest. In his other hand, he held out a cross. "You have no power here. I banish thee from this house and commit you to the shadows where you belong."

There was a sound to his right. Gideon saw Leighton, expression firm, also holding a cross. And across the room, Westaway stood at the window, a wild light in his unnatural eyes.

Gideon stared at him. What on earth was he doing? Blocking the exits?

I will have what I'm owed! The Collector had diminished in size, shrinking in on himself. He rallied, launching himself towards Gideon and Fairweather. *You owe me—*

"One who showed no mercy in life receives none in death." O'Connor advanced. "You are owed nothing. In the name of the father, son and holy spirit—depart!" He began a Latin chant.

The Collector hissed, a sound of pure fury. He flew at O'Connor.

"Look out!" Gideon flung out a hand too late.

The Collector's skeletal hand seized O'Connor's arm. He screamed. His bones collapsed into dust, joint by joint, suit dissolving likewise. With a vicious howl, the Collector dissipated into dust.

Gideon's hand closed on frosty air. Light flickered, the flames of the fireplace creeping back.

"I stand corrected." Leighton knelt, lighting a candleholder from the fire. As he raised it, Gideon saw again the walls and furnishings of the modern 32 Belcairn Road. "Some spirits are hostile. Are we sure it's gone?"

"It's gone," Westaway said, with a certainty that Gideon didn't think to question until many days later. "Lawes, any harm done?"

Gideon drew in a deep breath. He had been so certain of his demise it was strange to realise that he was as yet among the living. "I think not. I—" His head snapped up, scanning the room.

No sign of Fairweather.

"You gave us a nasty scare." O'Connor replaced the crucifix in his pocket and wiped his hands on his priestly vestments. "I shudder to think what might have happened if we'd been even a minute later." He nodded to Westaway. "Fortunately Julian noticed your absence and put two and two together."

Gideon took a step towards the place he'd last seen Fairweather, stretching out a hand. His fingers closed on nothing, not even a hint of cold.

"What gave you the idea that Lawes was in any danger?" Leighton asked. "You were very confident his unshakeable moral code would protect him."

"Every man has an exception." There was something strange in Westaway's tone.

Gideon looked up, but Westaway was eying his attire with dissatisfaction.

"Who allowed me to leave the house wearing a plaid vest and a checkered tie?"

"You seemed to think there was some urgency to the situation," Leighton reminded him. "Well, as our business here is done, I suggest we return to the house to congratulate ourselves on a job well done."

"No." Gideon's protest was raw. All three men looked at him, Leighton puzzled, O'Connor placid, Westaway with that strange remoteness that no longer bothered him. "The exorcism, you said it worked." He licked his lips, unsure how to phrase a question whose answer he feared. "Have all the spirits been banished?"

Westaway answered. "The only people in this house are the four of us. No one else."

27

"There were only ever two ghosts," O'Connor said. He sat in an armchair in Leighton's sitting room. "Holford's obsession with past wrongs consumed him. Fairweather's ignorance of the situation held the Collector at bay. In Fairweather's presence, Holford retained his sense of self. When Fairweather departed, the monster took over."

"Fascinating." Dr Harris's tone was rapt. "If only I'd been there."

"Consider yourself fortunate you missed it." Westaway sat on the floor, leaning against the sofa legs. "I lost my favourite pair of gloves in the excitement and tore my coat."

"You'll survive," Leighton said without sympathy. "Think about me. I had an actual haunted house, and now what do I have?"

"The undying gratitude of the landlord." O'Connor pointed out. "Hawarden wept when he heard the news."

"He wept when he realised he'd lost a guaranteed tenant," Leighton muttered.

Gideon stared at the floor. Holford had allowed him to see Fairweather that last time. He must have known what Gideon intended. The man was too intelligent not to. Why then had he granted Gideon's request? Had he believed that there was no way Gideon could free Fairweather? Or had the human part of Holford wanted to end the situation?

What difference did it make? Gideon rested his hand on Cleo's back. He would never know. Holford and Fairweather were gone. There was no coming back—for either of them.

"What now?" Dr Harris asked. "A poltergeist perhaps? Or maybe a headless coachman?"

Leighton snorted. "I intend to return to Foxwood for some recuperation. This has been most trying."

O'Connor smiled. "I'm headed to Epsom. Someone has to warn Wiremu against the dangers of gambling."

Dr Harris turned his gaze to Westaway and Gideon. "I suppose we must look to the younger generation to continue the pursuit of the unknown?"

"Unknown nothing," Westaway said. "I'm pursuing a decent valet."

"No difficulties there," Dr Harris said. "Go to Harbinger's employment agency. The chap's got an answer to every servant problem."

Gideon's mouth twisted. Harbinger's! How long ago that seemed now.

"What are your plans, Mr Lawes?" O'Connor asked.

"Oh, he's joining us at Foxwood," Leighton said. "You will come, Mr Lawes?" He looked so positive, it was impossible to say no.

Impossible, but somehow Gideon managed it. "Your invitation is very kind, but I'd prefer to stay in London and concentrate on my search for employment."

Leighton's eyes sparkled. "If you're searching for a job, Mr Lawes, I direly need a secretary—"

"You direly need restraint." Westaway elbowed his father. "Lawes has had enough of the supernatural. He has no desire to traipse through abandoned houses, do you?"

Should he feel flattered that Westaway was on his side—

or stung that he didn't desire Gideon's presence at Foxwood? Gideon smiled. Somehow, Westaway's behaviour did not rile him as it once had. "Westaway is right. I'm looking for something more mundane. I was considering education."

Dr Harris snorted. "You'd be safer with ghosts."

"Teaching," Leighton mused. He poked Westaway. "Who was that bright young chap who came to ours for Christmas that once? He was going into teaching."

"Halifax," Westaway said. "You remember him, Lawes. He's ensconced at a boarding school in Devon. I'll write, see if he knows of anywhere with an opening."

Westaway was as good as his word. Halifax replied in the affirmative. There was a hasty shopping trip (Westaway declared Gideon's wardrobe inadequate), an interview with the headmaster, and an offer. Two weeks after the exorcism, Gideon stood on the platform of King's Cross station, a suitcase in hand, Cleo's lead in the other. Two travelling trunks stood on the platform beside him.

Westaway leaned on a polished walking stick as he checked the time on his pocket watch. "Not long now."

"It's good of you to see me off." Gideon winced. Everything between them, and he couldn't get past such commonplace statements.

"Nonsense," Westaway said. "You know it's my pleasure."

Gideon believed him. "Why?"

Westaway looked at him. His eyes held no resentment or even surprise at the question. "I don't think you realise it, but you are extraordinary, Lawes. In your own way."

Gideon smiled with surprise. He had not felt very merry these last two weeks. "Says you." He hesitated. "Westaway, have you ever considered—" He stopped. What exactly was he asking?

Westaway looked down at his watch. "It would never work." He raised the watch, making a show of squinting at it. "You are too meticulous. You'd need to understand me, to know where I was and what I was doing. I don't want to be understood. I just want to be." He dropped his watch into his pocket. "Your train approaches."

"So it does." Gideon snapped his fingers. "Here girl." He scooped up Cleo. "I don't know how to thank you."

"Then don't." Westaway tugged at the sleeves of his perfectly fitted suit. "I'm going to be personal, Lawes, but you really shouldn't thank me. I don't think you've noticed, but I am bored, lonely and sick of my own company. In short, I'm in dire need of a friend."

Gideon blinked. "Ah."

Westaway reached out, giving Cleo's ears a scratch. "Don't be a stranger." He turned, walking away.

Just when he thought he'd figured Westaway out... Gideon shook his head. The train rolled to a halt, and passengers and porters swarmed forward. With a firm grip on Cleo, Gideon braved the crush.

Westaway had shouted him a private compartment and Gideon sank onto the seat in relief. Cleo sniffed all the corners of the compartment before jumping up onto the seat next to him. Gideon stroked her ears. "Better not let the ticket conductor see you do that."

He unfolded his newspaper and spread it out to read.

In no time at all the grimy streets of London gave way to the open vistas of the countryside. Gideon watched a forest go by with a twinge of regret. Perhaps he should have considered Leighton's invitation. Foxwood Court, from the sounds of things, was well endowed with forest...

He glanced down at the newspaper and got a shock. Someone had scrawled over the article he'd been reading in pencil.

Conductor in the next carriage.

Gideon looked at his hand clasped around a thin pencil stub left in his coat pocket. He had no memory of reaching for the pencil.

He swallowed, not daring to hope. "Fairweather. Is it you?"

The reply was immediate, his hand firm despite the swaying train.

Were you expecting someone else?

Gideon's eyes welled. He could not read the paper, his eyes full. "Fairweather, I—"

His hand moved again. Gideon dug a handkerchief out of his pocket and wiped it across his eyes before he could read the words.

Bedivere. Please.

He felt a slight presence to his right, a cold tickling pressure on his arm. For the first time since the exorcism, Gideon smiled with his whole heart. "Bedivere."

Gideon sat at the front of his classroom. Before him, twenty-four neatly groomed heads bent over their exercise books. The only sounds were those of pencils on paper, the occasional sniff, or the rustle of fabric as a student shifted in his chair. To all appearances, 4-B was focused on the task set them by their new arithmetic master.

Gideon was not fooled. He shifted the exercise book he was marking to one side and let his hand rest on the notebook he always carried.

His hand moved immediately.

Maywater (second row, the boy with ink on his blazer) is cribbing off the chap in front. Holmes and Meredith (fifth row, centre and centre right) have smuggled in a stink bomb and are planning to lob it at the sandy-haired chap in the front row.

Gideon cleared his throat. "Holmes and Meredith, there are to be no stink bombs in my classroom. If I see you with one again, I will confiscate it. Is that understood?"

The class blinked in astonishment, then craned their necks to look at the guilty parties. They sunk into their seats. "Yes, sir."

"Good. Maywater, your parents didn't send you to school

so you could copy off your fellow students. I'm assigning you a second page of exercises to do in prep—and do by yourself. No one is to help you."

"But sir—"

"I mean it, Maywater. You're here to learn how to think for yourself. Or would you prefer two pages of exercises?"

That math question was well within Maywater's grasp. "No sir. One is enough."

Gideon permitted himself a slight smile. "Good. As a reward for working so well, class is dismissed early. Mind you're quiet in the hallway."

The boys were silent until they reached the corridor. "How the devil does he do it?" Holmes complained. "The man's uncanny!"

"Spooky," one of his peers agreed. "Eyes in the back of his head? Wouldn't surprise me if he had eyes in the walls."

Gideon snorted and shut the classroom door. "Little rotters." His tone held affection. The boys, when they weren't plotting mischief or trying to get one over on their masters, were affable. Teaching was not the chore he'd feared. The moments when he saw comprehension bloom across one of the student's faces gave a real feeling of accomplishment.

He sat down at his desk and picked up the pencil.

Toads, Fairweather agreed. *Still, we've got their number.*

"Thanks to you." Teaching was new enough that his stomach fluttered at the start of every class. Knowing Fairweather was there, even if he couldn't see him, was a substantial help. "The next period is free. I'll get this marking done, so we'll have the evening to ourselves."

Fairweather didn't protest. Out of the corner of his eye, Gideon saw the novel he'd confiscated from a sixth former flutter open, the pages turning. Smirking to himself, he turned his attention to his student's work.

Some of his students were as hopeless with figures as Fairweather, but most had enough knowledge of mathematics that Gideon finished his task with time to spare. He joined the boarders for dinner, supervised the juniors at their prep, and took Cleo for her usual night time walk. She was proving a great favourite with the boys.

Gideon climbed the stairs to his quarters with anticipation. As a new master and a junior one at that, his apartment was tiny, consisting of a sitting room with a partition for his bed and another for his washstand. The housekeeper had apologised for its size, but Gideon had assured her it was more than adequate. There was room for a bookcase, a desk and two armchairs before the fire.

"At last." He pulled off his jacket and hung it up, following it with his tie. Cleo made a beeline for the rug laid out in front of the blazing fire.

The rattle of the tea tray let him know that Fairweather was resident. A whistle called his attention to the kettle boiling away on the fireplace. "Allow me."

He poured the boiling water into the tea pot and stood the kettle on its stand. Heavy objects or delicate manoeuvres had given Fairweather some difficulty at first, but he'd mastered manifesting enough to take charge of making the tea. Gideon watched the floating teapot pour two cups.

He took out his notebook and balanced it on his leg, letting his writing hand relax. "At the risk of tempting fate, I'd say this is going well. Would you agree?"

The pencil slid across the paper. *If anyone deserves a bit of luck, it's us,* Fairweather replied. *How fortunate the previous arithmetic master retired.*

Gideon pressed his lips together. "Very coincidental, don't you think? That the arithmetic master at a school where one of my Balliol friends teaches Classics suddenly calls it a day. Do the boys know anything about it? From what I've gathered, his retirement came as a complete surprise to the staff."

There's a rumour to the effect that your predecessor—who was rather too free with the cane, in the students' opinion—received payment for past wrongs in the form of a visit by a monster. Fairweather could apparently carry on a conversation while manipulating objects. One teacup and saucer floated over to Gideon.

He took his cup. "A monster? They can't believe that."

Opinion in the fifth and sixth form is that he misjudged his drinks. The fourth plump for a prank and are desperate to discover the perpetrators. Third form is divided between a subconscious manifestation of the master's own guilt and bank robbers in disguise, while the first and second formers are firm in their belief that a half-man, half-beast monster terrified him into leaving his position.

"Half-man, half-beast." Gideon snorted. "What is the education system coming to?"

You're the education system now.

"There will be no monsters in my classroom," Gideon said. "Just good honest ghosts." He raised his teacup. "To friendship."

Fairweather's cup clinked against his. He saw the cushions in the second armchair move as Fairweather resettled himself. Gideon sipped his tea. He didn't need to see or touch Fairweather to enjoy his presence.

When Cleo had warmed herself to her heart's content, she settled herself on his lap. Gideon set his empty teacup down and stroked her ears. He glanced at the other armchair.

"Bedivere…"

I'm content, I assure you.

Was he so transparent? "I know this isn't the life you're used to. My circumstances are very different and I'm a dull chap—"

The pencil flew across the paper in rebuttal. *Believe me, I have had more than enough of the high life! After so much time confined, you do not understand the interest I find being out in the world again. Though the boys, amusing as they may be, do not hold a candle to their master. I don't mind where we go, so long as you're there.*

Gideon blinked. He felt the temperature lower, and a light pressure at his eyes. He closed his eyes and placed his hand over Fairweather's. It was easier to feel him when he could not see. "I do not deserve this wonderful fortune, but I'm so happy I do not care." Bedivere was with him, with him and happy to be with him. "Your companionship is everything I never knew I missed."

He felt a slight pressure on his shoulder, but the pencil remained still. Had he flummoxed Fairweather?

A fluttery touch against his forehead. Gideon's cheeks heated. Fairweather's kisses never failed to fluster him. *And your regard everything I never knew I wanted. Shall we leave it at that?*

"Have it your way." Gideon did not mind losing this argument. He felt the cool pressure of Fairweather's fingers on his and curled his hand around them. Was it his imagination, or was Fairweather's presence growing more distinct? "To think none of this would have happened if Westaway's valet hadn't walked out on him."

A most peculiar man. Do you think he'll ever find a valet that will suit him?

Gideon smiled. "Stranger things have happened."

EPILOGUE

Firelight flickered over the armchairs in the drawing room of Foxwood Court. Not the formal drawing room reserved for visitors, but the smaller room that had done service as Pip's study. Pip much preferred it to the larger, more formal room, which seemed too large without Cross's expansive presence. He rested his cup of tea on his knee, regarding the other armchair's occupant. "Heard from Lawes recently?"

Julian turned the page of the novel he was reading with marked indifference. "That depends on what you mean by recently."

"I saw you had a letter from Yorkshire last week."

"He's arrived at his school and is settling in."

"And?"

"And that was it." Julian turned another page. "Lawes is not what you'd call an expansive letter writer."

Pip weighed his son. "Have you replied to his letter?"

Julian looked up from his novel. "Father."

"It would be polite to acknowledge the receipt of his letter, that's all." Pip took a sip of tea and counted to twenty under his breath. The important thing was not to seem too eager.

The other important thing was to make sure Julian knew what an opportunity he was losing. "Lawes is a very nice young man."

Julian snapped his novel shut. "I know what you're thinking, and no. I have no complaints against Lawes as a companion, but that is as far as it goes."

"But he's so suitable," Pip protested. "Much more suitable than other friends you've had." Julian looked up, a combative glint in his eyes. Pip hurried on. Better to avoid the subject of Julian's previous friendships. "And you have so much in common. An education, a common circle of friends—"

"He's my class, you mean." Julian rolled his eyes. "Your prejudices are showing, oh paternal one."

"I am only thinking of your happiness." Pip motioned to the room they sat in, taking in the bookshelves, the comfortable armchairs, the warm fire. "How do you expect to settle down with a labourer or an itinerant street performer?"

Julian curled in his armchair. He reopened his novel, searching for his page. "That was years ago. A youthful infatuation."

"Not that long ago. I was embarrassed for you. I'm still embarrassed."

"If you were embarrassed, you'd let the matter rest."

"Marco the Magnificent." Pip snorted. "What was so magnificent about him?"

"He was a strongman," Julian said without looking up from his book. "Have you ever met a circus performer who didn't bill themselves as some variety of superlative?"

"An oaf with an over-developed physique, and that was it. I don't know what you ever saw in that lout." Pip huffed.

"His moustache. You must admit, it was remarkable."

Pip eyed his son with displeasure. Julian was not reacting

appropriately to his thoughtful paternal care. "He looked like a walrus."

"Perhaps that was part of his appeal."

Pip slammed down his cup of tea. "Now you're just being facetious. I'm trying to have a serious chat with you, and you're ruining it."

"It won't work." Julian uncurled himself from his chair and stood. He ruffled Pip's hair. "You cannot fuss me into happy domesticity, no matter how hard you try."

"Is it so wrong to worry about you? I was your age when I met Thomas. All the happy years we spent together here…" Pip looked at the fireplace, his eyes growing misty. "I won't be here forever. And when that day comes—"

Julian's fingers tightened on Pip's shoulder. "You're not to be morbid." His tone was light, but not convincingly so. "We both know that you're not going anywhere, not until you've got your proof of ghosts. There will be plenty of time for you to deplore my taste in friendships yet."

He should not have smiled. He was trying to instil Julian with a proper appreciation of the fleetingness of life and its opportunities, and Julian was not cooperating. "I don't know what I will do with you."

"Shake your head at me and tell me how many grey hairs I've caused you." Julian retrieved his novel and flipped through it, searching for his page. "That's what you usually do."

"So you do listen?" Pip cocked an eyebrow. "Then while I have your attention, turning into a wolf to escape unwanted visitors was immature when you were eleven, and is decidedly passé now that you are a grown man." Pip paused as Julian dropped his novel and turned to face him. "If you turn yourself into a wolf to escape me, I shall—"

"Send me to my room without supper?" Julian's eyes glinted with amusement. "It's all right you know, father." He looped his arms around Pip, leaning against him as he'd done as a much younger child. "We're both going to be all right."

Bother Julian! Pip wiped his eyes. "If Thomas were here, you'd listen to him. He always knew what to say."

"If he were here now, you know what he'd tell you." Julian lowered his voice, adopting a wry tone. "Julian does things his own way, in his own time. Let him figure things out for himself."

"That's a dreadful imitation. I hope you haven't been listening at doors. That's a very common habit." Pip tried to look stern.

Julian snorted and released him. "I don't think you appreciate quite how good my hearing is. Goodnight, Father. It's too nice a night to spend indoors. I'm going to walk in the woods."

"Mind you stay in the park," Pip said. "And don't go after the neighbour's rabbits. One of these days, he will take a shot at you and then where will you be?"

"Fuss fuss fuss." The door swung shut behind Julian.

"I don't know why anyone bothers having sons." Pip settled back in his chair, watching the flames.

The devastating absence had faded to a dull but steady ache. He could look at his grief now as a part of himself, as much a part as his love had been, see in Julian's more frequent visits home his own grief too. It did not ease the pain, but knowing it was shared made it easier to bear.

Julian does things his own way, in his own time. It was exactly what Thomas would say too. Pip sighed. It wasn't the same as hearing from him...

Pip leaned on his stick, heaving himself out of his chair. He settled himself at his desk. Julian said he had no complaints against Lawes as a companion. What could be more companionable than an invitation to Foxwood Court? He placed a piece of paper on his blotter and picked up his pen.

My dear Mr Lawes,

It would give Julian and myself much pleasure to invite you to spend the school holidays with us at Foxwood Court...

ALSO BY GILLIAN ST. KEVERN

August 2020

The Disturbance at Foxwood Court

There's no Royal Society for the Protection of Werewolves.

Taming a stray dog was supposed to occupy Pip while he recovered from illness—not embroil him in a chilling supernatural plot. Nothing in his occult library explains how to care for a juvenile werewolf, but Pip knows this much: he would sooner die than let Julian be recaptured by the sinister Professor Rathbone.

He might have to. Rathbone will let nothing interfere with his experiments. To save Julian, Pip must risk his life, his reputation, and the world he's built with Cross.

The Disturbance at Foxwood Court is the tenth book in the Read By Candlelight series, a collection of gothic novellas that weave suspense and paranormal mystery around an evolving ensemble cast. Preorder The Disturbance at Foxwood Court today to dive into a world of suspense, the supernatural, and proper table manners.

To be first to read *The Disturbance at Foxwood Court*, support me on Patreon. Alternatively, stay up to date with my news and future releases by signing up to my newsletter. Alternatively, you can preorder it on Amazon.

THE WING COMMANDER'S CURSE

An unbreakable curse.
England overrun by monsters.
Two men locked in a losing battle.

England, 1915.

Jonah Valliant longs for active service, but is stuck making coffee for the local officers. A year ago, the world erupted into magical chaos. No one knows why Britain is overrun by fearsome worms, magical creatures whose gaze turns men to stone, or how to stop them. When Jonah loses his temper with Wing Commander Mallory, he has no idea that picking a quarrel with the wizard may lead to Britain's salvation—or its destruction.

Augustus Mallory carries more than the weight of the war effort on his shoulders. He's the last of the Mallory wizards, feared for their power, arrogance and the dark family curse. Losing his heart to Jonah endangers everything Mallory cares about, but Jonah may possess the key to defeating the worms once and for all. Mallory's only hope: staving off his doom long enough to learn the dreadful truth behind the Quickening.

Sign up to my newsletter for your free copy of The Wing Commander's Curse.

BOOK REC: SHADES OF SEPIA

There is a story behind this rec. Basically way back when I still lived in Japan, I'd just completed the first draft of my contemporary vampire urban fantasy/paranormal romance, and was wondering if there was a market for it. I googled and found my way to the homepage of Shades of Sepia's then publisher. The book caught my eye, and when I saw that one of the main characters was a kiwi, I had to get it.

I could not believe this book. Main character called Ben? My book had a main character called Ben. Ben was a DCU geek? I was writing Young Justice fanfic! When Ben's ringtone turned out to be my favourite Dave Dobbyn song, I messaged a friend to share the coincidences. She asked me if I was sure that I hadn't written the story myself.

As I kept reading, the sense of familiarity grew. More and more I was reminded of my friend Anne who had taken me under her wing when I first poked my head into fandom. We'd fallen out of touch since then, but I still had her email address. I emailed her, asking if she'd seen this book. She replied, 'I wrote it.'

Anne and I have been back in touch ever since, beta-reading for each other, supporting each other on our writer journeys and founding The New Zealand Rainbow Writers together. Anne's releasing *Shades of Sepia* ahead of a return to this world and I could not be more excited about it.

To be soulmates they first have to survive.

A serial killer stalks the streets of Boggslake, Ohio. The victims are always found in pairs, one human and one vampire.

Simon Hawthorne has been a vampire for nearly a hundred years, and he has never seen anything like it. Neither have the other supernaturals he works with to keep the streets safe for both their kind and the humans.

One meeting with Simon finds Ben Leyton falling for a man he knows is keeping secrets, but he can't ignore the growing attraction between them. A recent arrival in Boggslake, Ben finds it very different from his native New Zealand, but something about Simon makes Ben feel as though he's found a new home.

After a close friend falls victim to the killer, Simon is torn between revealing his true nature to Ben, and walking away to avoid the reaction he fears. But with the body count rising and the murders becoming more frequent, either, or both of them, could be the killer's next target.

Author's note: This story was originally released in 2014 by another publisher. This edition has been revised and re-edited with the end result being a better, stronger story.

Find Shades of Sepia on Amazon.

ACKNOWLEDGMENTS

Very special thanks to my Patreon supporters for their continued encouragement: Jennifer, Julia, Kathleen, Khadija, Lexy, Patricia, SpookMouse, Theanna and Y Lee—you rock! Thank you!

Another thank you to Anne and Sera for reading, and Sera's editorial suggestions—as always, your help was invaluable at keeping me on track and my commas under control.

ABOUT THE AUTHOR

I realised I wanted to be an author when, as a teenager, I found myself getting annoyed that the characters in the books I read weren't doing what I wanted them to do. Now that I'm a writer, they still don't.

I write a variety of genres, ranging from short and silly contemporary romances to urban fantasy and mystery. My current project is the *Read by Candlelight* series of gothic romances inspired by the works of M R James, J S Le Fanu and the Brontë sisters.

In my non-writing life, I live in my native New Zealand, where I enjoy flat whites, playing pretend with my niece and nephew and trying to keep up with my ever increasing to be read pile. I'm the co-founder of the New Zealand Rainbow Romance Writers.

If you enjoyed *The Collector* and want to leave a review, I will be so excited, I may just spill my tea.

gillianstkevern.com
info@gillianstkevern.com

www.ingramcontent.com/pod-product-compliance
Lightning Source LLC
Chambersburg PA
CBHW032025050726
47590CB00006B/2303